The unauthorized reproduction or distribution of a copyrighted work is illegal. Criminal copyright infringement, including infringement without monetary gain, is investigated by the FBI and is punishable by fines and federal imprisonment.

Please purchase only authorized editions and do not participate in or encourage, the piracy of copyrighted material. Your support of author's rights

This book is a work of fiction. Names, characters, places and incidents are the product of the author's imagination or are used fictitiously. Any resemblance to actual events, locales, or persons, living or dead

Bound: Masters of the Savoy copyrighted 2022 by Delta James

Cover Design: Dar Albert of Wicked Smart Designs

Editing: Michele Chiappetta of Three Point Author Services

Want FREE books from Delta James?

Go to https://www.subscribepage.com/VIPlist22019 to sign up for Delta James' newsletter and receive a copy of *Harvest* along with several other free stories. In addition to the free stories you will also get access to bonus stories, sales, giveaways and news of new releases.

❀ Created with Vellum

BOUND: MASTERS OF THE SAVOY

A SUPERNATURAL MYSTERY AND ROMANCE

DELTA JAMES

ACKNOWLEDGEMENTS: *These things are so hard to write. It can't be as long as the book, but you fear leaving people out. So instead, I'll just go with the basics:*
- *To my father who gave me the gift of storytelling*
- *To Renee and Chris, without whom none of what I do would be possible*
- *To the Girls: Goody, Katy, Emma, Roz, Ava and Skylar*
- *To my ARC, Critical Reader and Focus Groups, JT Farrell and all of my readers – thank you from the bottom of my heart*
- *To Michele Chiappetta of Three Point Author Services, Editor Extraordinaire for all her hard work and putting up with my crazy schedule*
- *To Dar Albert of Wicked Smart Designs, the genius behind my covers who works with nothing from me and produces the most amazing artwork, which then become my covers*

CHAPTER 1

*T*ime. He always thought there would be more time. Each time when a small part of him escaped the trap of the crystal caves located below Tintagel, he had less and less time before being sucked back in. He only dared to venture out to keep Britannia from falling, but the forces of darkness were ever present, and he could do little more than react to the threats as they presented themselves.

London, of course, had not existed when his king had reigned, but the capital as it had been then had faded into the mists of time. London was now the capital, which made it the heartbeat of Great Britain. He had been surprised when he'd ventured out to find that the dark forces had built a portal from their world to the real one under the veritable noses of those who should have been most concerned. He'd managed to cast a spell so that their gateway would only open if the great clock struck thirteen times. Then and only then would the pieces of glass that formed the face open and allow something truly wicked to enter the world.

Fortunately, he'd been able to create and put into place four great guardians of the city—four enormous lions that would come to life when the clock struck thirteen. Each time, the beasts had joined forces with one of his descendants, who would lead them in battle, force them back behind the veil and seal the rift that had allowed them to come forward. Those warriors were descended from his loins and carried the spirit of the eagle.

The responsibility had now fallen upon one who did not believe. A girl who had not a clue about her heritage or her destiny. She would need to open her eyes to all that was around her and call upon all of her gifts and knowledge to defeat the evil thing that was coming. He feared what would come if she did not rise to the occasion.

One Year Ago

As Corinne left the Savoy, her mobile rang.

"Corinne Adler?" said the voice on the other end of the phone.

"Yes, this is Corinne."

"Your aunt has asked for you. I know it's frightfully early, but your aunt has taken a sudden turn for the worse. I'm afraid she doesn't have much time left…"

As she headed out the door, Corinne realized the voice had to belong to her aunt's newest caregiver, Delores. "No need to worry, I was just getting off my shift. Do I have time to stop by my flat and change?"

"I would think she has several hours yet, but she is adamant that she must speak with you."

"I should be there easily within the hour."

"I'll let her know. My sympathies for your impending loss."

Corinne rushed home, grabbed a quick shower and a change of clothes, and headed to her Aunt Peggy's flat. Her aunt was the veritable black sheep of the family. No one but Corinne had spoken to her for well over a decade. Choosing to not upset her parents, Corinne had refrained from mentioning that she and her aunt had been in regular contact for the last several years.

It wasn't that Corinne didn't recognize her aunt's deteriorating mental acuity. At first, she'd tried to convince herself that her aunt was simply becoming forgetful, but finally her aunt confirmed that she had been diagnosed with Alzheimer's sometime back.

"It will kill me in the end," Aunt Peggy had said. "I'd always hoped I would die fighting with the boys, but then that was selfish of me."

Corinne had wondered who *the boys* might be and

why her aunt thought she would die fighting with them, and against who. The Alzheimer's had taken its toll, and her aunt's mental and physical health was failing. Pneumonia had finally begun its deathly crawl through Aunt Peggy's body. When Corinne had questioned why her aunt seemed unwilling to treat it aggressively with antibiotics and settled instead for palliative care, the doctor explained that most in the medical profession called pneumonia "the terminal patient's friend," as it would allow them to slip peacefully away.

Within an hour of taking the call, Corinne was knocking on the door to her aunt's flat. A small, round woman with a kind smile, which didn't quite reach her eyes, opened the door. Corinne assumed this was her aunt's newest hospice worker. She was older than Corinne and younger than her aunt.

"Corinne? I'm Delores. Your aunt has been asking for you."

"Is she in much pain?" she asked as she spoke with the woman in her aunt's living room. "What should I expect?"

Delores took Corinne's hand in hers. "She isn't in any pain and seems peaceful and resolved. The pneumonia is progressing as expected, but we have her on oxygen, so she isn't struggling to breathe. As for what to expect, death should claim her easily. Each case is different, but most likely she will either take one last deep breath, expel it and be gone. Or she'll slip away so quietly, you won't even notice… until you do. It shouldn't be traumatic so if you can't stay until the end, just let her say what she needs to and then I'll get you out."

"No. I want to be with her. I've called my supervisor to let him know what's going on. Spense is a great guy and told me that he'd ensure my shifts were covered. I want to be here with her until she passes. I don't want her to die alone." Corinne shook her head. "I'm sorry. I know you'd be here, and she wouldn't be alone, but I want her to have family…"

Delores' smile was kind and full of empathy. "I understand."

When they walked into her aunt's bedroom, Corinne was surprised at how normal and pleasant the room looked. There was medical paraphernalia, of course, but her aunt's bed had been propped up and she looked like there was nothing wrong with her—tired, but not as though she were on the verge of dying.

Aunt Peggy's eyes lit up when Corinne entered. "I'm so glad you could come."

"Where else would I be?" Corinne said, leaning down to kiss her aunt's cheek. The skin felt as though it were delicate tissue that could rip and tear with little provocation. "I should have been here more often."

"Poppycock. You've been here at least weekly since you moved to London and every other day for the past three months. I know how busy your life is."

"Yes, but I'll be graduating next year…"

"But then there will be a new job in your chosen field. Your parents must be so proud. The first of the family to get a college degree."

Corinne laughed. "They'd much prefer I came home, married some local boy and settled down to have lots of babies."

A shadow crossed Aunt Peggy's eyes. "I fear that will never be your destiny. I pray you are luckier than I was and find someone with whom to share this terrible burden." She looked up at Delores. "Delores, darling, could you leave us? I need to speak to my niece about a private family matter."

"Of course, Peggy. I'll be in the other room; just call if you need me," Delores said as she withdrew, leaving her alone with Aunt Peggy.

The sudden weight of being the only family member to share her aunt's last hours on earth hit Corinne with the force and power of a mine cave-in. So many emotions assailed her, but she couldn't seem to find the words to express her feelings. Aunt Peggy was her mother's sister, but as far as Corinne knew, they hadn't spoken in over a decade.

"No time for reminisces, regrets or recriminations. I have so much to tell you. So many things you should have known in order to prepare, but the ravages of this insidious illness have caught me up, and there's no more time." Aunt Peggy smiled. "He always said that regardless of how much time we had, it was never enough. I have been given this gift of a period of lucidity before my end. You must listen to me. You must believe me," she insisted.

"Aunt Peggy…"

"Promise me, Corinne. Promise me you will believe me and will continue studying with Holcroft."

Steven Holcroft was a sword master of some renown. Many actors had learned the art and discipline of the sword and other ancient weapons from him. Corinne had been surprised when her aunt had taken her to his fight studio, introduced them and then demonstrated her skill.

"Aunt Peggy, I've always listened to your stories. I've tried to believe, but you have to admit some of them are a bit out there."

"I know, baby, but you must believe. I know your parents warned you away from me. Your mother thinks our legacy to be a curse as it took our mother away from us. I'm sure every instinct tells you that I have Alzheimer's and that my fantastical tales are nothing more than delusions, but they aren't. I swear to you, the stories, our family's lineage and legacy are true. You must pick up the sword and answer if destiny calls on you." Peggy seemed to run out of breath, coughed, but prevented Corinne from calling Delores. "Have you been keeping up with your lessons?"

Corinne knew she didn't mean her college courses. "Yes. Last month I moved from sabers to broadswords. Holcroft was resistant to letting me advance, but in the end I convinced him, and he agreed to keep teaching me. I've gotten really good with the bow. The quarterstaff and halberd are more problematic for me, but I can use both. Can I ask why any of this is so important?"

Aunt Peggy nodded. "Under the bed, you'll find two wooden cases with handles."

Corinne knelt on the floor at her aunt's side and pulled out the two cases. They were rectangular in shape, not overly deep and had intricately carved lids.

"Got 'em," Corinne said, opening the larger of the two and gasping.

Inside was a bow and quiver. The quiver was made of a butter soft leather decorated with a carved dragon design. It held a bundle of arrows, each with a tip of engraved silver. Beneath the quiver lay a bow made of what appeared to be yew with an engraved obsidian grip. The limbs of the bows were also capped in obsidian. One end was a carved dragon's head and the other end, the dragon's tail.

"You are looking at Storm Shadow. She has been passed down through the female line of our family since the time of King Arthur. It is said that Merlin imbued the bow with the power of light and that it can defeat the darkness. The arrows have been made by the same family of fletchers since the Normans invaded England."

"Merlin? As in King Arthur and Camelot?"

The corners of Aunt Peggy's mouth lifted into a wan smile. "One and the same. We can trace our female line back to him. In each generation, one daughter is chosen to stand as the Sentinel of the Portal. Your grandmother was the Sentinel before me, and you have been chosen to be the one who follows."

Corinne leaned forward. "Was that the argument that made you leave?"

"Do you remember that?"

"Only that you argued. I remember a lot of raised voices—and then you were gone."

"Your mother did not want you called and blamed me for not having daughters of my own. But once you were born, I knew you were the one."

"How did you know?"

"The birthmark on your shoulder blade. The one that looks a bit like a sword."

"Mom said it was hereditary."

"It is. And once I knew you had been chosen, I had hoped to live my life training you, but your parents wanted nothing to do with it and so kept you from me. I'm sure they weren't happy that you made contact." Her aunt paused, arching her eyebrow. "Do they even know?"

"I told them after we had brunch that first time. Mom seemed frightened and dad was furious. It seemed easier not to bring it up. I did let them know when you went on hospice…"

Her aunt laughed. "And they said *good riddance.*"

Corinne smiled. "They weren't that bad…"

"Keep in mind, my dear girl, you can go to hell for lying as well as stealing."

"It bothers me that I'm the only one here."

Her aunt waved her hand, dismissing her concern. "It would have been hypocritical of them to have showed up. You should know, I never held anything against them and when the time is right, you should tell them I forgive them. Now, open the other box."

Corinne closed the lid to the case that held the bow and the quiver of arrows. If the bow had caused her to gasp, the object that lay encased in the velvet lining of the second box rendered her speechless.

The double-edged, silver blade gleamed with an almost ethereal glow. The gorgeous metal was engraved with what Corinne could only assume were detailed Celtic runes and symbols. The obsidian pommel had been carefully carved in the shape of a snarling dragon to match Storm Shadow. The grip was wrapped in black leather, the guard an ornate filigree of silver.

"Pick it up," rasped her aunt, her voice growing weaker.

Corinne raised the broadsword. Power surged up from the grip, infusing her system and humming through her body, giving her a life and energy she had never known before.

"What the hell was that?"

"Galatine has accepted you."

"Galatine?"

"The sword," said Aunt Peggy.

"How do I know that name?"

"Galatine is the sister sword of Excalibur, given to Gawain by the Lady of the Lake. Merlin retrieved it before it fell into the wrong hands or languished back into obscurity. It was Merlin who passed it down through the ages."

"What am I supposed to do?" Corinne asked, pleading for an understanding of what was expected of her.

"The faces of Big Ben are made up of pieces of cut glass, not a single plate."

Why is she telling me this?

"When the clock strikes thirteen..." Aunt Peggy continued.

"Clocks don't strike thirteen."

"Never say never," quoted her aunt. "It has only happened a few times since its creation. The tower itself was built over a portal into a demon dimension. Each time the gateway into this world has started to crack, a woman from our family has acted as Sentinel and has called forth the lions at the base of Nelson's statue in Trafalgar..."

"How do you expect me to do that? Call, 'Here, kitty, kitty, kitty'?"

Peggy's brief laughter caused an eruption of coughing. "No. They each have a name—Nelson, Wellington, Victory and Napoleon. When the clock strikes thirteen, tap the nose of the lion on the corner closest to Big Ben—that's Wellington—and call him forth. He will awaken and call to the others. They will follow you to fight the demons and keep them from escaping into the world."

"Assuming that ever happens, then what?"

"The Sentinel's job is to keep the demons at bay and force any who try to make their way into this world back through the portal until it re-seals itself. The entryway will only be open for thirteen minutes and then it will close again."

"What if one of these things gets through?"

"Then you and the lions will have to destroy it. The lions and Storm Shadow can wound them, but only Galatine can kill one—and only then if you cut off its head."

"Will the lions know they are supposed to do what I tell them?"

"Yes, they will do your bidding. When you kill the demon, it will vaporize completely. Swear to me you will answer the summons should it ever come."

Corinne placed Galatine back in the case. Her aunt had to be delusional, didn't she?

"I don't want you to go. I want more time."

"Time. It has been the bane of our family. There is never enough. Promise me you will continue to train. Never stop. You must be ready. The vigil and duty to protect this world from those who would come through now falls to you." Aunt Peggy's grip felt surprisingly strong as she squeezed Corinne's hand. "Promise me."

Delores must have heard her aunt's voice raised in desperation, for she re-entered the room just as Corinne found herself forced to make her decision.

Corinne grasped her aunt's hand in both of hers. "I will, Aunt Peggy. I will." Aunt Peggy nodded, smiled and relaxed against the pillows, the life draining from her eyes. "Aunt Peggy?" she cried as her aunt's body went limp.

"She's gone," said Delores, confirming her words by taking her aunt's vital signs. "The responsibility now falls to you. Are you ready?"

CHAPTER 2

*P*****resent Day***

Corinne Adler opened one eye as the alarm clock on her dresser went off. The late afternoon sun filtered through her gossamer drapes. It wasn't as if she didn't have an alarm on her phone, but her phone stayed by her bed. The old digital alarm with its annoying beep sat atop her dresser, across the room so that she had to get up to shut it off. The damn thing continued its obnoxious siren's call to get her ass out of bed. She grabbed one of her pillows and threw it at the dresser, managing to knock over a lamp and a necklace hanger—completely missing the offensive object.

Resigning herself to the inevitability of having to get up, she threw the covers back, swung her legs over the side of the bed and stalked across the room, managing to stub her toe on the end of her bed.

"Shit!" she growled, finally reaching the alarm clock and pressing the reset button... But still it continued to bleat at her. She hit the button a second time; the clock bounced but continued to squawk.

Corinne grasped the back of the clock, grabbed the power cord, and jerked it out of the wall. Blessed silence. She stumbled into the kitchenette of her small studio. It was all she'd been able to afford when she was attending college, studying history with a special emphasis on British myth and legend. Her aunt had left everything to her. So, she'd sold Aunt Peggy's flat, paid off her student loans and now had enough left over to finally purchase a flat of her own. She had her eye on Rachel Holmes' old flat in Charing Cross. It was a large airy space filled with light, and Corinne had been there a few times and loved both the location and the ambience.

She sliced the supposedly pre-sliced bagel and slid it into the toaster. *Why do they say they're sliced when they aren't?* It popped up just as she got her first cup of coffee. Seeing the pale, barely browned bread, she wondered why toasters never toasted anything right on the first try. The second go-round proved to be perfect, though, and she slathered the bagel with butter and apricot jam before heading over to her one small window that overlooked the Thames and Trafalgar Square beyond.

Lord Nelson stood in his heroic pose, the four Landseer Lions resting at his feet. Corinne could no longer look at them without wondering which name went with the other three lions. After all, she knew which one was Wellington. She slumped down in the chair, watching people crawling all over them, although they weren't supposed to. Smiling into her coffee mug, she wondered what they might do if Big Ben ever struck thirteen times and one or more of the lions came to life.

For that matter, what would she do? Her Aunt Peggy's last hours had been spent spinning some wild tale about the lions coming to life and Corinne having a mystical destiny. According to her aunt, if Big Ben were ever to strike thirteen times at midnight, Corinne was to take the sword that now resided under her bed, go to Big Ben, and tap the nose of one of the lions to bring him to life so she and all four lions could fight one or more demons trying to escape into the world. The sword was supposed to be a magickal sword passed down through generations of the women of her line. Magickal sword? What a load of poppycock!

Aunt Peggy had been adamant that the monarchs of England believed that if Big Ben ever struck thirteen times, then each of the seven-ton statues would come to life and devour the city. Thus, the reason each monarch ensured that an entire team was in place to safeguard the clock and its workings. According to her aunt, the legends were wrong. The lions weren't supposed to consume the city, but rather stand with the Sentinel of the Portal to protect

London from whatever was trying to come through the Veil. Aunt Peggy had said that upon her death, Corinne would be the next one of their family to assume that mantle.

According to her aunt, the Landseer Lions were only the most recent representation of the great beasts that protected the city. A long line of warrior women descended from Merlin had been the guardians and masters of the creatures—to stand with the beasts if the forces of evil sought to come through the Veil to destroy the city. Corinne shook her head and reminded herself that her aunt had been a victim of Alzheimer's, but she'd used her last breath to impart what she felt was vital information. The last thing she'd done was exact Corinne's promise to take the bow and sword and be prepared to defend the capital.

Corinne glanced at her clock. *Shit*! Her day was not getting off on the right foot. Corinne hustled into the shower and got dressed quickly, leaving her flat, trotting down the stairs, headed for the Savoy. She loved her job. Even though her aunt's claims to a family legacy had been hard to swallow, Corinne had still arranged her life according to her aunt's wishes. She could see Trafalgar Square from where she currently lived, and both her home and work were close enough to get to Big Ben in a hurry if she needed to. When she bought her own flat, she would ensure that its location fell within those parameters.

Arriving at the Savoy, she stopped by the

concierge's station to look at the schedule before checking in with the front desk. Spense wasn't there, which most likely meant he was in his office.

"Evening, Corinne," said Brenda, one of the hotel's front desk staff.

"Hey, Brenda. Is Spense in his office?"

"Yes. Just tidying things up in there and getting ready to head home."

Corinne stopped and looked at her. "What's the goofy smile for?"

"Funny how these days Spense is much more inclined to get out of here on time."

"I know. I try to tell myself it's envy that I feel and not jealousy."

"You need to get a man on the side," said Brenda.

"I need to catch my breath. I just finished my final exams earlier this week."

"Congratulations!"

"Don't jinx it. I won't get my grades for at least two weeks."

"But you know you passed. What's your degree in?"

"British Myth and Legend."

Brenda giggled. "Still trying to find out about our ghost?"

"Ghosts? We have several. Curiously, not much is known about them—especially the little Victorian girl in the yellow dress. It's almost like someone way back then was trying to cover up something."

"Well, I would think that here in jolly old England, there's plenty of source material."

"Not as much as you might think—at least not written down. Most of it is recorded oral stories handed down in families. Every time I think I've got a piece of it, it slips through my fingers."

"I daresay your family didn't engage in such nonsense," said Brenda.

"You'd be surprised," quipped Corinne.

She walked down the short hall to Spense's office, knocked and stuck her head in. "Hi, boss. I checked the desk; it looks like a quiet night."

Spense looked up and smiled. "Yes, just the Hendersons. They're here on their honeymoon and are headed to the West End for a show. I upgraded them to the Rolls limo. Saoirse and I are meeting with Roark, Sage, Gabe and Anne for a drink before we meet with Rachel and Holmes at the Coal Hole."

Corinne sighed. "I'm going to miss Watson, and the Savoy won't be the same without Roark and Sage. Everything is changing. Even me. I'm graduating. I think it's probably time I find a place that isn't over a curry restaurant."

"But an excellent curry restaurant," noted Spense. "Keep in mind, the only constant in life is change."

"And what's the old Chinese curse? May you live in interesting times. By the way, don't think that anyone here hasn't noticed all the changes you've made since you and Saoirse got together. She's good for you."

She and Spense were more than supervisor and employee. Granted, she wasn't as close to him as the close-knit group of friends that made up his inner circle, but certainly much closer than most.

"She makes me incredibly happy, and I now understand why Roark, Holmes and Watson were all so keen for me to find a woman of my own. I can tell you she was worth the wait. I know you're graduating soon. Management is wondering if you're planning to stay on."

"For the foreseeable future. I'll have a doctorate, but there's not a lot of call for someone with my degree except in teaching, and teaching is just not something I want to do… at least not right now. I applied for one job I really want, and they've made me a provisional offer, but it's only part-time. Could you do me an enormous favor, and let Rachel know I'd like to talk to her about her flat?"

"I can do that. Are you interested in buying or leasing? I don't know that she's made a decision either way about what she wants to do with it, but I think if it were you, she'd be open to either. You didn't ask, but I think it would be a lovely place for you. Close to everything that's important to you, including the Savoy. I'll have her get in touch with you."

Corinne went into the employee locker area, stashed her gear, pinned on her name tag, and headed out to start her shift. The Savoy was special to her, as was her work, and there was a part of her that couldn't imagine not being here. The fact that the National Gallery even had an opening had been exciting. That they'd offered her a job dependent upon her earning her doctorate had sent her over the moon. Besides, the flat in Charing Cross, the National Gallery and the Savoy Hotel made a nice little triangle for work and living.

She reminded herself that she didn't believe her aunt's tales of demons trying to enter the world through Big Ben or the Landseer lions coming to life or that she had descended from the great wizard, Merlin. But from the moment he'd learned her aunt had passed, her weapons instructor had been training her more intensely. She often found herself standing at the window in her flat gazing at the lions, watching to see if they would move, which was utterly ridiculous.

Corinne dragged her thoughts away from her musings and focused on the job at hand. She helped get the Hendersons situated with their driver. They were delighted and very appreciative of the upgrade. That was something she'd learned from Spense, that making people's stay at the Savoy just a touch more decadent took very little effort and expense. She began going through the updated list of guests—who had come in, who had left, and who would be coming and going the next day.

She looked up to see the three couples leaving the hotel to meet with their friends for dinner. Corinne had to admit, if only to herself, that she would enjoy having a man in her life in general and especially if they could fit in with that small, intimate group. It wasn't that they were exclusionary, just tight-knit. They were the nicest group of people. They seemed to have a depth of trust and friendship that was greater than most. And the four women of the group —Sage, Rachel, Anne and Saoirse—were troublemakers of the first order but seemed to have such a good time.

At first, she had found the dominant personalities of Roark, Holmes, Watson and Spense a bit overwhelming and hard to take. But the more she got to know them and saw how they doted on the women in their lives, the more she wondered if they weren't onto something. None of those women had any fear of the men and were treated with a level of respect that was something to be envied. In fact, she'd talked briefly to Sage about how Roark was able to lift a lot of the day-to-day responsibilities from her so that she could focus on her writing. Corinne realized that what she really wanted was to be able to share her life with someone, talk to them about what her aunt had told her, but she was fairly sure that, like her aunt, she would remain single.

Corinne shook her head to clear it of her musings. She didn't have time for a man or for close, intimate friendships. According to her aunt, she had a destiny and must be prepared to act if Big Ben chimed thirteen times. She'd been training most of her life. She was adept with sword, bow, quarterstaff and halberd. The reason for the training had seemed silly, but it was good exercise and a lot of fun—besides, she excelled at it. She told herself that if Big Ben ever did sound the warning, she'd be prepared. Then, all she had to do was retrieve her magickal weapons, tap the nose of a seven-ton bronze lion and make their way from Trafalgar Square to the Queen Elizabeth Tower without being seen or causing a panic while she fought some demon trying to enter this realm. *Simple, right?*

Corinne got up and made a round through the halls of the hotel. During the day, the hotel's concierge was kept busy helping guests, arranging tickets, giving information, ensuring the hotel's car service was scheduled correctly. But at night, demands for the position died down and she had more time to herself. The hotel was hers to roam as long as she had her comm link with her and open.

Rumor had it that somehow Spense—she smiled as she really liked that Saoirse had renamed him—and his friends had somehow found out who the little girl in the Victorian dress was and had helped her spirit find peace. That sounded like that group. They always seemed caught up in some mystery or another. It would be nice to have a group of friends with whom she could share adventures. Her aunt's claims notwithstanding, Corinne led a somewhat dull life. It was busy, but not necessarily exciting. Up until recently she'd been busy with school, her duties at the Savoy and her training.

At the end of her shift, Corinne checked out with Spense and then headed for home. She walked to the tube station and then stopped at one of the local fresh air markets to pick up vegetables as well as artisan breads and cheeses. Meat, fish and poultry were never a problem. Her immediate family was made up of fishermen, farmers and butchers. She received cryo-packed beef, pork, fish and poultry from her family at least monthly. She was fairly sure that she was one of the few people who lived in a studio flat who had a chest freezer.

Big Ben's thirteen chimes were the harbinger that something evil was about to make its way into the world through the clock face, which was said to be a window into the Veil—a place where time had no meaning, good and evil were engaged in an eternal battle, and magick ruled. Scary stuff if you were to believe in such things. Luckily for Corinne, she didn't.

Or did she?

CHAPTER 3

Merde. Eddy now understood the hell Sage had put Roark through when Roark was still trapped within the pages of Sage's novels. Corinne was going to drive him crazy. It seemed that every time he thought she was safe—unlike the situations his friends put themselves in—Corinne found a way to put herself at unnecessary risk.

She wasn't off fighting the Angel of Death or calling the banshees to banish Jack the Ripper to hell or freeing the spirits of five little girls from the curse of a malevolent spirit. No, Corinne just did small, silly things that could get her hurt or worse. For instance, she rode the tube late at night or early in the morning when Spense had told her repeatedly the hotel would happily supply her with a ride to her less than desirable neighborhood.

Ever since his old friends left the confines of Sage's manuscripts, Eddy hadn't been able to talk to them face-to-face, but he still found a way to communicate. At first, they'd been limited to emails, but then Eddy devised a way for them to use both instant messaging and texting. The ability to communicate with his friends in real time, like having the ability to keep an eye on Corinne, made his half-life within the pages of the books less lonely.

Eddy:Damn it, Spense. Taking the tube at that time by herself is dangerous.

Spense:Agreed, but she refuses when I offer.

Eddy:Then insist.

Spense:I do. But I can only push so hard. It's not like we're involved in a romantic relationship. We're colleagues and friends to a certain extent. I've told her I wish she would take a cab or have one of the drivers take her home, but she's very independent.

Eddy:She has some interesting hobbies.

Spense:Such as?

Eddy:Sword fighting, archery, working with both a halberd and a quarterstaff, and then of course she's a runner.

Spense:That is odd. Have you ever done a deep dive on her?

Eddy:Yes, but there's nothing really to know about her or her immediate family.

Spense:What about her not-so-immediate family?

Eddy:She had an aunt who seems to have been estranged from her family for more than thirty years. When she died, she left Corinne everything. She had the same hobbies. The information about the aunt is rather sketchy with lots of holes. I'm trying to track them down.

Spense:We can all try to keep better tabs on Corinne for you, but as you know, Anne and Gabe are immigrating to America and Roark and Sage have moved out of the hotel.

Eddy:I know. And I know Corinne is an adult and is quite capable, but I just have this feeling. Did you know she got a job at the National Gallery? It's part-time and she's planning to stay at the Savoy.

Spense:Maybe it's time for you to come out…

Eddy:It's never something I saw myself as doing, but maybe…

Spense:I used to worry that we would be sucked back in. Now I worry more that somehow, whatever window was opened and allowed us to escape will close and you won't be able to get out.

Eddy:Who says I want to?

Spense:I don't think Corinne could join you. Even if she could and she wanted to, would you allow her to?

Eddy:You have a point. I'll think about it, but I worry I wouldn't be able to help all of you if I was out there.

Spense:Sage wrote you as a genius and a

legendary hacker. So far, all of us have come through the Veil with our talents and skills intact. Besides, there isn't a one of us who doesn't want you out here with us in the real world.

Eddy: Thanks, Spense. I'll think about it. My best to everybody else.

Screen Blips Off

Eddy stared at the blank screen. It had been an odd thing becoming sentient. At first, it had felt disconcerting and a little frightening. But those feelings had lessened as he realized his friends had experienced the same thing. Losing first Holmes and Spense and then Roark as they pierced the Veil and entered the world, Eddy had begun to wonder if maybe he wasn't cheating himself.

CHAPTER 4

*E*ddy watched Corinne sleep from behind the Veil. It had long ago ceased to surprise him that so many people slept with their laptops open. It took some skill to be able to use someone's personal computer to watch over them. *Watch over...* Yeah, he used to think when Roark did it with Sage it was a bit stalkerish, but now the shoe was on the other foot. It seemed like the right thing to do.

He couldn't help but compare his relationship with Corinne with Roark's relationship with Sage. They were very similar except for the fact that he didn't have a connection yet with Corinne. The unfortunate fact was, she didn't even know he existed. Like Roark, Eddy was separated from the woman he wanted by the Veil—the woman for whom he had developed very strong feelings.

Of course, Roark had been able to pierce the Veil

in order to save Sage's life. Holmes and Spense had sort of tumbled through the Veil a short time before Roark. None of the three of them understood how it had happened, and they no longer seemed to care. Eddy didn't think he could ever trust, much less enjoy, something he couldn't understand. The others were so nonchalant, they drove him crazy.

At about the same time as Holmes and Spense disappeared from the pages of the manuscript, Eddy had felt a pull—something akin to having a lasso tighten around his middle, trying to draw him through the Veil. It had been as if some force was compelling him to let go of what was and embrace the unknown. But he hadn't been sentient as long as the others and felt he'd be of more use to his friends on this side of the Veil if he remained behind.

While that had been true, it wasn't the only reason he'd resisted being drawn into the real world. Eddy had liked being behind the barrier, securely experiencing the sort of half-life they had all enjoyed together in the pages of Sage's manuscripts. But there was another part, a murkier part, of his soul that reveled in his ability to connect with the dark web on a more visceral level.

In the beginning, he told himself staying behind was noble. But as he saw his friends evolving and enjoying rich lives, he wondered if fear wasn't really at the heart of his resistance. His reasons to remain on the other side of the Veil were valid, and there was nothing to compel him to leave his safe little haven. *Safe*, that was the kicker. Did he want to stay safe, or did he want to embrace the possibility of a full life?

None of those things had mattered when he saw Corinne for the first time. He'd been talking to Spense when the attractive, blonde-haired, blue-eyed woman had appeared over his shoulder, checking in for her shift. She'd been dressed in a nondescript dark suit which did nothing for what he now knew to be a curvaceous figure—not overweight, but shapely and strong. She wore her long hair up in a messy bun, and her eyes most often danced with mischief.

She had captured his imagination, and from that point forward he'd been intrigued. Curiosity may have killed the cat, but it was a hacker's catnip. Eddy had gone browsing in the Savoy's computerized personnel records to get her mobile phone and address. Once he had those, it took little time for him to hack into her phone and then into the electronic devices in her home. At first, Eddy told himself he was keeping an eye on someone who could expose his friends, and then someone who was important to them, but had finally been forced to admit, it was because she'd become important *to him*.

Eddy was now willing to admit that there were things he knew about Corinne that he didn't share with his friends, but then he suspected there were things they didn't share with him about the women they loved. Loved? He resisted labeling his feelings as love, but he wasn't sure he could defend that position. Some of the things he knew about her were personal and endearing; others were odd and a bit concerning. For instance, she took regular lessons in ancient weapons like the bow, quarterstaff, halberd and broadsword. Why?

The first and last hadn't exactly surprised him, as she had two cases she kept under her bed that contained what he thought was the Storm Shadow bow and Galatine. At first, he'd chalked her training up to an intriguing form of exercise, but when he'd glimpsed the two weapons, he'd known better. Eddy had hacked into the fight master's studio and watched her lessons. She was good—almost as if she'd been born to it. Steven Holcroft was a fight master with impeccable credentials and a murky past that even Eddy had been unable to resolve. But he had to admit, Holcroft brought out the best in her.

Corinne's aunt had been a puzzle. Eddy liked solving puzzles and so had begun to dig up any and all information he could on her. The woman had managed to live off the grid in the middle of London—leaving no electronic trail, unless you knew how to find and follow one. Trying to track her financial records had led him through a tangled system of accounts until he'd finally found the source of her income. The woman had lived frugally, working as an artisan for Boodles, one of the most exclusive jewelers in England. But there had been other money coming in from an obscure and ancient organization known as the Order of the Seven Maidens.

The organization seemed to be a collection of women, spanning a wide range of ages and all from the most ancient families of Cornwall. They did some quilting and crocheting, but most of their services were direct and out in their community—helping the sick, bringing meals to those in need, tutoring and the like. So, Corinne's family was from Cornwall, but that didn't answer the riddle of why the organization was supporting Corinne's aunt.

He also couldn't figure out where the organization was getting all its money, and there was an inordinate amount of it. Eddy had tried to trace the origins of the money back through time but had become lost in a maze of accounts. Each month, the Seven Maidens had sent Corinne's aunt a sum of money to cover her living expenses, including the mortgage payment for her flat close to Trafalgar Square.

Peggy had left Corinne a large inheritance that had shocked Corinne, both in its size and scope. Eddy knew it came as a complete surprise. He'd been able to watch her reaction to the news—various phases of shock, excitement, confusion, strategic planning, disbelief and finally acceptance. Corinne's reaction had been to sell her aunt's flat, pay off her student loans and then buckle down to finishing her degree. Her final doctoral thesis had been turned in and she had interviewed for a part-time position with the

National Gallery and had been offered the job on a provisional basis. As long as she received her degree, the job was hers.

Eddy had watched as she bought her own bottle of champagne, cheese and crackers and celebrated by herself sitting by the window that looked across the Thames to Trafalgar Square. There had been a sadness there, and yet an acceptance. He wondered if she had resigned herself to living the same kind of solitary life that her aunt had lived.

Corinne's shock when money to cover her living expenses had been deposited to her account was comical and palpable. Eddy had been expecting it, but when the Seven Maidens had deposited the money into her account, she'd been surprised and called the solicitor for the estate. He had explained it was part of her inheritance and that additional amounts would be deposited as her expenses increased.

For the past few nights, her sleep had been broken and restless. Eddy could tell she was awake, as her movements beneath the covers were more deliberate than languid. Corinne flung the covers off, revealing she slept in the nude. More often than not, in fact, she chose to sleep without anything on. Eddy was glad of that. She had a lovely body, and he enjoyed seeing her. Enjoy might not be the best description. She aroused him, and he refused to take refuge in any of the non-sentient females that littered Sage's Clive Thomas novels.

Corinne lay in the middle of her bed, the cool night air making her sensitive nipples pebble. Eddy had observed enough to see how easily they responded to just about any kind of stimuli. Cold, the friction of rough material rubbing across them, a sex scene from one of Sage's books—all made her large, dark nipples go from soft to hard in an instant. She rolled the dark tips between her fingers and thumbs, sighing contentedly as she did so.

Eddy's eyes were riveted to her other hand as it trailed down past her mons, parting the petals of her sex to drag her honeyed essence from her core back up to play with her clit. *Naughty girl!* He had decided when she became his—wait, when had if become when?—that she would not be allowed to pleasure herself unless he commanded her to do so. Corinne moaned in need as she spread her legs further. God, how he wanted it to be him, spreading her thighs, making a place for himself between them. He felt a sharp stab of jealousy when he wondered who she fantasized about when she played with herself.

Corinne circled her clit with her moistened finger and dragged it across the swollen nub. He knew that some would consider him a pervert for watching her playing with herself, but Eddy didn't care. Everything Corinne did called to him. He realized he watched her giving herself pleasure so that he would already know how to make her relax and respond to him.

Her finger skimmed over her sex as she left her nipples and brought that hand down to join the other. Tracing circles around her clit with her index finger, she used the fingers of her other hand to splay her labia, exposing her beautiful pussy which glistened with the evidence of her need. Arousal hummed through her body, making it sing in a language that was as old as sin. A song that caught him up and made him forget everything but the beauty of the woman before him.

Corinne rolled to her side, opening the cabinet door of the table beside her bed. She brought out a wand vibrator and turned it on, allowing it to further stimulate the bundle of nerves at the apex of her sex as it peeked out from under its hood. As she let the sex toy do its job, she brought the other hand back up to play with her nipples—rolling, pinching and tugging. Her hips rolled in a language as old as time.

She pinched her nipples hard as she turned up the vibrator from a gentle buzz to something far more intense. Eddy longed to be providing her with that stimulation himself, before reaching under her, cupping the globes of her ass and steadying her as he mounted her. He wanted to thrust up into her hard and sure, hearing her gasp before she cried out.

Releasing her nipple, Corinne reached down and stroked her finger up deep inside her sheath. She worked her hands in concert, her breathing becoming shallow and thready—just this side of a pant—as she stimulated her sex. Throwing her head back, he watched her muscles tense as she increased her pace in order to bring on her orgasm. Corinne cried out as her climax washed over her. She seemed to revel in her pleasure. Eddy was certain that he could enhance and increase that pleasure so that she came more than once.

His cock throbbed, hard and uncomfortable, as he held it in his hand and began to stroke it with a firm grip. The damn thing had already been dripping precum. This wasn't going to take long. Eddy watched as Corinne used her hands to soothe the remaining fire in her blood and picked up the pace. He closed his eyes, imagining her tight sheath wrapped around his cock, spasming all along his length. He imagined her calling his name as his cum rushed up from his balls and spewed out, covering his hand. He pumped his staff until he was empty, and his body relaxed.

The alarm on the dresser across from her bed beckoned her to open her eyes. Her response as usual was to throw something at it. She actually hit the reset button more often than not. Knowing she wanted to get up at the time she'd set the alarm for, Eddy simply triggered the alarm again. He felt it was helpful but was also willing to admit he found it humorous.

"Shut up," she growled as she stretched her arms over her head. Eddy turned the alarm off, chuckling as that brought her up short and she looked at the device. "What the fuck?"

Eddy had to agree with Roark. Corinne's language, like Sage's, could use some looking after. He wondered how she would respond if he took her to task over it. The idea of pulling her over his knee and spanking her pretty ass until it was a bright shade of red was arousing and brought the dominant side of his nature to the fore. He'd never had much interest in truly dominating a woman… until now.

∽

It stood erect on its cloven hooves and pushed at the Veil with its hands. Its minions had been steadily weakening it for decades. Finally, the barrier between the two realms was beginning to soften and become spongy. Growing weaker. When the great sorceress opened the Portal, they would be ready. The time was coming when it would be able to push through the barrier that separated its dimension from the real world.

Real world? Bah. It would remake it in its own image. Slaughter, cruelty and chaos would reign. The Sentinel of the Portal had passed some time before. It wasn't sure exactly when, as time passed differently here in the realm of demons than it did in the land of humans. But it couldn't have been that long, and she'd had no spawn. The crones to the south would not be able to react fast enough to his entering the world to stop him. By the time they knew what was happening, it would be too late.

The first order of business would be to secure Galatine and any of the other swords that had belonged to the knights of the king that was and would be again… But no, that king would not return again. Not if Dragar had anything to do with it.

CHAPTER 5

Corinne needed to get a more reliable alarm clock. She felt certain she had hit the reset button with the throw pillow from her bed. But as it often did, it switched off and then went back to blaring at her until she got up and turned the damn thing off. She stretched her arms over her head as she swung her legs over the edge of the bed.

After grabbing a quick shower and getting dressed, she headed out into the early afternoon sun and headed for Charing Cross, excited to meet Rachel at her flat to talk about buying it. Rachel was waiting as she walked down the charming street.

"Corinne, it's so good to see you," she called with a friendly wave. Rachel was one of the nicest people Corinne had ever met. She was dressed fashionably in trousers, a silk tunic and flats—simple but elegant.

"Thanks for meeting me. Sorry I'm not more put-together, but I'm going to work out this afternoon before going to the hotel. How did the tour with the Hendersons go?"

"No need to apologize; you look fine." She smiled. "The Hendersons are a lovely couple. We did a tour of the Tudor palaces. I think when they started, they thought Henry VIII was a great king."

"I hope you disabused them of that notion. For someone who didn't major in history, I love how much Anne knows about him and that she has nothing kind to say about him."

"I have a doctorate in history, and I can tell you, Henry was a monster. But enough about a dead monarch. Let's go up to the flat. I'm so glad you're interested in it."

"Do you want to sell or lease?" asked Corinne.

"In all honesty, it doesn't really matter to me. Holmes says he's fine with whatever decision I make. Given that, I'm more concerned about who will live here rather than whether I sell or lease or even what I get for it. It may sound silly, but this flat is important to me. It helped me move my life forward when I could have just settled. I'd love to see it be important to the next person— not necessarily in the same way, but that they, too, see it as a place that made a difference for them. I will let it sit empty if I can't find the right person for it."

Corinne smiled, feeling as though the day was

taking a definite turn for the better. "So, you'd be open to selling to me?"

"I can't tell you how happy it would make me to see you take it."

They entered the building and took the lift, which was a converted freight elevator to the top floor, where the flat was located. Rachel opened the door and stepped back, allowing Corinne to precede her. Corinne couldn't help but feel as though she were coming home. It was as if the flat was making her welcome—offering her that same promise of solace it had given Rachel.

"You feel it too, don't you?" whispered Rachel.

"I do… like this is where I'm supposed to be. I'd forgotten that the whole back wall was windows and French doors."

"The doors lead onto a private balcony. When the developer converted the place, they opened up an atrium at the top, so even though it looks onto the interior common space, it's quiet, lets in a ton of sunlight and lots of fresh air."

"As I was coming up from the tube, I tried to tell myself that I couldn't be remembering how much I liked it here. This was my dream flat from the first time I saw it. I think maybe that's why the decision to sell my aunt's place was so easy."

"I think sometimes, the right places sort of let you know. When I found this place, I bought it on the spot. But once Holmes showed me his family home—

now our home—I knew that's where I belonged. But I don't want you to feel pressured to take it," confessed Rachel.

Corinne nodded. "Something like your place with Holmes is far too big and far too grand for me. I love this place—all that light from the atrium and a private patio."

"It is lovely. I've already taken the things that I want from here, so anything here you'd like to have, we can include with the deal."

Corinne turned, looking at the bed, and sighed. "My place came furnished and not with the best of furnishings. I did buy myself a good mattress and disposed of the old one. I told my landlord when I moved, I would leave it. Going from a double bed to a queen would be another upgrade."

"I renovated the kitchen, bath and closet last year. The original bath was cavernous," Rachel said, leading her toward that side of the flat to show it off. She opened the two doors, turning on the lights. Corinne all but gasped. "By stealing some of the space from the bath and just a smidge from the kitchen, I was able to give myself a walk-in closet. I had one of those closet systems installed. It was the first thing I did at the townhouse. Holmes thought it was silly and unnecessary, but once I had it done, he had to agree it was the right thing to do."

Corinne entered the relatively large walk-in closet with rows of hanging rods, drawers and shelves.

There was also a lovely full-length mirror hanging on the back of the door.

"Before I fall in love with this place, what are you asking for it? My aunt left me some money and if I can swing it, I'd prefer to buy."

"Holmes and I talked about it. He suggested getting it appraised and using that as the basis for the price. Honestly, Corinne, I'd love to see you get it. I think it would be perfect for you. I know Spense would love to see you in a better, safer neighborhood. Holmes and I are prepared to finance it for you as I own it outright."

Corinne whirled around. "Seriously?"

"Absolutely. I remember what it was like getting my doctoral degree, paying off student loans, getting a job, all of it. It's not like we don't know you, and we'd like to lend a hand if we can. Spense said you've had an offer from the National Gallery."

"I have. As long as my degree comes through. It'll only be part-time for a while, but I figure getting my foot in there is the way to go."

Rachel nodded. "Come on, let me show you the rest of the place. You probably don't need a guide; it's not huge."

Corinne laughed. "Are you crazy? It's at least double the size of the place I rent now, and it doesn't smell of curry."

Rachel showed her the bath. "I love a good soak after a hard day. I found this antique slipper tub and had the bath built around it. I had a separate shower put in with dual shower heads and a third hand-held one. Probably overkill for the size of it, but it has killer water pressure and feels so good. And I have a tankless hot water heater, so no worries about running out of hot water."

"God, Rachel, this place is so much better than I remembered. I love the beams and high ceilings."

"When I was looking, I actually came to see one of the ground floor units, but this one was available as well and once I saw it, there was no contest. As with any studio, it's very open concept. I did upgrade the stove and fridge, and there is a pull-out pantry."

Corinne stuck her head in the pantry, offering plenty of space to store things. "This is perfect. I'll have to figure out where to put my chest freezer, but with this big fridge, I might not even need it."

"You have a chest freezer?"

"My family is in Cornwall—butchers, farmers and fishermen. I get packages of meat, poultry, pork and fish on a regular basis. My dad is convinced I'll starve, because nothing in London can compare to their fresh meat. I have to say he's right." Corinne turned around slowly, taking in the flat in all its glory. "I would love to take you up on your offer to let me buy it."

Rachel clapped, delighted. "I'm so glad! We'll have to get all the legal stuff done. How much notice do you need to give?"

"Virtually none. I'm on good terms with my landlord; he knows I've been looking, and he has a waiting list of students."

"Then if you like, ask him if the last day of the month will work for him. You can move in, and we'll get all the paperwork done as quick as we can."

"That would be amazing."

Rachel extended her hand. "Then you just bought yourself a flat in Charing Cross. Here's your key. I have to run as I've got a tour starting. Why don't you make a list of anything you want to keep over the next few days, and let me know. We'll get the rest moved out."

Corinne shook her hand. "Thank you so much. I just love it, and the location is great for me."

"Not a bad place to start a life with someone," teased Rachel.

Rolling her eyes, Corinne said, "Don't you start. I get enough of that from Sage and Saoirse."

Rachel laughed and headed out. Corinne closed and locked the door behind Rachel and then squealed as she twirled around. She hadn't been kidding. Compared to her flat over the Indian restaurant, this place was huge. It had plenty of storage, and Rachel had done all the expensive upgrades, all of it beautiful because Rachel had exceptional taste.

After taking it all in again, Corinne glanced at her watch. Ah, she had just enough time to grab a bite to eat before heading over to her archery lesson. So, she double-checked to make sure the French doors were locked, set the alarm and then let herself out.

After grabbing a bite to eat at a nearby pub, a place she was sure would become her new favorite, she raced to Holcroft's and took her place among the other archery students. Holcroft had converted his studio from an enormous warehouse along the industrial area on the Thames. Its cavernous space featured ample areas for fencing, archery and other ancient weapons. It also included a regular gym where his employees taught self-defense and a running track suspended from the ceiling—perfect for staying in shape.

"Remember," the fight master said to the group, "you draw with the strength of your core, not your shoulders. Watch Corinne. If the rest of you put in as much archery practice as she does, you'd hurt yourselves if you didn't do it right."

"Teacher's pet," whispered one of the other students, an actor in a miniseries that was set to premiere soon on the telly.

"Damn right she's teacher's pet," said Holcroft. "She's also been a student here for quite some time and is one of my best pupils. You just need to be able to look like you know what you're doing. Corinne here can actually hit a bullseye ten out of ten times. Isn't that right, Corinne?"

"Only because of your excellent instruction." She turned to the rest of the students. "He sometimes forgets that when I first started, I punched myself in the face more often than not."

The class laughed.

"But she kept coming back," said Holcroft. "Kept practicing. Kept listening. Corinne has a regular membership here, and I generally see her at least six days out of seven."

"What he's trying to say," said Corinne, "is I have no life."

Again, laughter erupted.

Even Holcroft chuckled this time. "Or a secret life none of us knows about. I'll tell the lot of you this, if there's ever a fight and the Queen wants to know who London's best archer is, I know who I'm nominating for champion."

Holcroft led the class off the firing range as Corinne watched, leaning on her bow. Now, what had he meant by that? It wasn't the first time he'd made some kind of reference to her being London's champion or savior.

She'd brought a change of clothes with her and so slipped into the shower after her training. It wasn't anything fancy, but at least there was a dedicated space for each gender. She'd always loved taking showers here as the water pressure was incredible and seemed to have endless hot water. According to Rachel, she would have the same in her new place. She leaned her head against the back wall and let the hot water pelt down on her back, moaning as it unkinked the muscles. By the time she'd finished, her aching core and fingers felt much improved.

After getting dressed, Corinne headed out, grabbed some street food for an early dinner and began to make her way to the Savoy. Seeing as she had the time, she headed for Trafalgar Square. She watched as tourists played on the Landseer lions, which they were not allowed to do. With a sigh—knowing people just don't do what they're told—she approached the lion her aunt had called Wellington and stood looking at him for the longest time.

"Sometimes, I almost expect them to blink or shake their heads or something," said an elderly woman who had wandered over to study the statue with her.

The woman seemed to be the epitome of the quintessential English woman *a la* Joan Hickson as Agatha Christie's Miss Marple in her signature skirt, blouse, tweed jacket and coordinating hat.

"I know. Me too. I often wonder what it is they see," said Corinne.

"I like to think they're keeping watch over the city. There's a legend that says they may one day come alive and devour all of London."

"Only if Big Ben strikes thirteen times at midnight. Actually, there are two legends," Corinne explained. "One which casts them as the villains and the other as heroes."

"What do you mean?"

"One says if the clock strikes thirteen, the lions will come alive and destroy the city. The other is that if that happens, it means London is in danger and the lions will awaken and rise up to defend it."

"Do you believe that?" the elderly woman asked as Londoners and tourists alike milled all around them—talking and snapping photographs.

"I like to believe that if some great evil were to arise, the lions would come to our defense. I wonder if that isn't why there are four of them, each looking in a different direction."

"Has Big Ben ever struck thirteen?"

"They say only a few times, and each time was a bad omen. I know the last time was during the Luftwaffe air raids."

"I lived through that," the old woman said. "Trust me, if there'd been giant bronze lions roaming the city, we'd have known."

"Maybe," said Corinne. "Or maybe not—because it was at night, and everyone had their blackout shades and curtains in place."

The other woman chuckled. "You might be right. I remember there was some talk that some of the buildings that were destroyed didn't look like they'd been bombed, just crushed."

Corinne smiled and headed on her way. *Interesting conversation,* she thought as she made her way to the Savoy and a busy evening catering to a large group of Sherlock Holmes aficionados. When they announced they were headed for a private tour of 'Baker Street,' she had to suppress a laugh. She hoped it was the tourist attraction dedicated to Sir Arthur Conan Doyle's famous detective and not the BDSM club that shared the almost identical address. Otherwise, the group dressed in their Victorian finest was in for a big shock.

CHAPTER 6

*E*ddy had, at Holmes' request, begun to regularly monitor the security system at Rachel's old flat. He'd been running a routine check when Rachel had shown Corinne the space. He'd been relieved when they'd struck a deal for Corinne to purchase it. It pleased him that she'd be living in a flat with its own alarm system in a secure building, much safer that her current digs.

But it wasn't Corinne's new lodgings that had kept him awake the last few days. He'd begun picking up chatter on the dark web about something going down in London. Not a terrorist attack; not even something of the real world, but something from another dimension planning to try and break through. Eddy tried tracing the bits and bytes he'd picked up but kept running into dead ends. Normally that wasn't a problem, and he could work his way through or around them. But every time he tried to track down this particular information, it was as if a gigantic wall crashed down, stymieing his ability to find out what he wanted to know. At first it had been irritating, but now it was becoming alarming.

Eddy:Saoirse? Are you there?

Saoirse:I'm here, Eddy. What's up?

Eddy:I'm not sure. I know you have some gift of foresight.

Saoirse:Are your spidey senses picking up something too?

Eddy:So, it's not just me.

Saoirse:No. I've been feeling it too. Like something's going to happen. Something big.

Eddy:I've picked up some idle chatter, but it's not the usual terrorist or mafia kind of stuff, which I normally pass on to Holmes. It's more supernatural.

Saoirse:Same here. Something is unsettled. Something evil. Are you secure?

Eddy:Why do you ask?

Saoirse:Every time I think about you, I get the feeling the walls are closing in.

Eddy:I've been feeling just that. Like, in order for whatever this thing is to get through, it has the power to shut down any open portals around it to draw in their power.

Saoirse:Spense and I were going to contact you tonight. He thinks you need to get out. He thinks if you don't now, you may never have another chance.

Eddy: I'm not unhappy on this side of the Veil.

Saoirse: But 'not unhappy' isn't the same thing as happy.

Eddy: I'm useful here. I can provide support.

Saoirse: You can do that here as well. Eddy, I'm not one to tell people what to do, but I think you need to try and get out before something happens that prevents you from ever getting out.

Eddy: I'll think about it. Pass the info onto the others. Take care.

Saoirse: You too.

Screen Blips Off

Eddy spent the rest of the day trying to track down anything tangible on what seemed to be rattling both his and Saoirse's cages. The more he tried to pick up on threads, the more avenues he was cut off from. His chat with Saoirse left him unsettled. The more he thought about it, the more Eddy wondered if his friends on the other side weren't right. Perhaps if he wanted to escape from the pages of Sage's books, he needed to make plans to go now.

Saoirse was a powerful witch, and the things she saw with her gift were rarely wrong. Unfortunately, it dovetailed with what he'd picked up in the furthest reaches of the dark web. What was the old saying? *Something wicked this way comes.*

Corinne was just making notes from her shift when Spense arrived.

"I hear congratulations are in order," he said.

"You must have talked to Rachel or Holmes."

"Actually, Saoirse told me. In case you haven't figured it out, let me clue you in. If one of the four of them knows, they all do. I don't think I really want to know how much Sage, Rachel and Anne know about my sex life."

Corinne rolled her eyes. "Probably only about half of what you know about theirs."

"Not true. I think women are far more gossipy about things like that. Meanwhile Roark, Holmes, Watson and I live by the old adage that gentlemen never kiss and tell."

"You just keep telling yourself that, Spense. And you don't just kiss and tell; you go hang out together in a kink club."

"You've never been to Baker Street, have you?"

Corinne shook her head. "No, I'm not inclined in that direction."

"What direction might that be?"

"I'm not judging. I think whatever works for people and doesn't harm others outside that relationship is what they should do. But I am not submissive, and I just can't picture myself in black leather and boots wielding a whip."

Spense's smile wasn't at all condescending, but rather indulgent instead. "Forgive me, but I don't think you have an understanding of the lifestyle at all, or at least not the way Saoirse and I live it. I'm not trying to convert you, but before making up your mind, you might want to find out more about it from actual practitioners—not just what you see in films or read in books."

"I'm too strong to be a submissive… at least I like to think so."

"That's probably the most common misconception… You see, those who choose to submit—and that's the key word, choose—are among the strongest people you'll ever know. And there are plenty of Dommes out there. For us, it just helps us play to our strengths, define our own roles in the relationship and keeps the lines of communication open and honest."

Corinne stepped back, thinking about what he'd said. "I'd actually never thought about it that way."

"Whether or not you even choose to learn about it is, of course, up to you. But I think you'll agree that none of the four women you know who are subs would ever be considered weak."

She nodded. "That gives me something to think about."

"That's always a good thing. In any event, Saoirse wanted me to ask if you needed help moving."

The offer relieved her. She'd been dreading having to find a moving company.

"That would be wonderful. It shouldn't take long. My old place was furnished. I'm leaving the mattress I bought and the chest freezer. Mostly, I've just got personal stuff—clothes, dishes, stuff like that."

"One or two SUVs?"

"Two probably, or one if you want to make two trips. I'm planning to move next weekend. Do you want to get started early?"

"As early as you like. Shouldn't take us any time at all, and Saoirse said the girls would be happy to help you unpack."

"Perfect. Thank you so much."

She finished up her notes and clocked out. It had been a lively night so when she reached her flat, she was still wide awake. Her landlord had been happy enough to save sturdy boxes for her, and she began packing.

When her mobile rang, she answered.

"Dr. Adler?" asked a feminine voice.

"This is Corinne Adler. May I help you?"

"This is Gloria Burton at the National Gallery. I have a friend at your school, and she just confirmed you have passed all your classes and achieved your doctorate. Let me be the first to congratulate you on both your doctorate and hopefully your position here at the National Gallery."

"Really? Thank you! And if you're offering me the position, I would be happy to accept."

"Wonderful. Could you start on the first?"

"The tenth would be better for me. I'm moving

next weekend, and I'll need to know my hours at the museum so I can work out a schedule at the Savoy."

"Do you think that'll be an issue?" asked Dr. Burton.

"Not at all. The hotel is very accommodating, I just want to give them a little time to get it figured out."

"Very commendable. The tenth it is. Shall I change the address for your personnel records?"

"Yes please," Corinne responded, giving her the address to her new flat in Charing Cross.

"I know that neighborhood. In fact, I think I know that building. Do you know Rachel Moriarty? No, wait, it's Holmes now. I thought it was humorous that she was changing her last name from Moriarty to Holmes."

"I know Rachel fairly well. It's her flat I'm buying."

"Oh, I am now pea-green with envy. I've been there a few times. Gorgeous place."

"I know. I'm very excited."

"Good enough. We'll see you on the tenth. Come in through the employee entrance. One of the security guards will bring you up to my office, and we'll get you settled in."

"Sounds perfect, Dr. Burton…"

"Gloria, Dr. Adler."

"Good enough, Gloria. It's Corinne."

"Good luck with your move, and I'll see you on the tenth at nine."

Corinne ended the call and hugged herself. It seemed her hard work was paying off. As she had a dedicated parking space, maybe she'd think about getting a vehicle of her own. Not an SUV, too big, but one of those Mini Coopers might be fun.

Knowing she had a lot of work to do in the next couple of weeks, Corinne got right down to planning. She made herself something to eat and began a list of things to do. One of the tasks she needed to accomplish was to buy some appropriate work clothes for the museum. On something of a whim, she dialed Rachel.

"Rachel Holmes. Oh, hi, Corinne, I didn't look at the caller ID first. How are you?"

"Excited. I just talked to the National Gallery. My new boss found out I have been awarded my doctorate, so she confirmed her job offer. I start on the tenth."

"That's wonderful news on both fronts. We should all go out and celebrate."

"That would be terrific, but I was wondering if I might impose…"

"Impose away. I understand from Saoirse we're helping you move. And Spense was right—we'd love to help you unpack."

"I would appreciate that more than you know. But

I was wondering if you might go shopping with me. I've worked at the Savoy, and that's one look…"

"Oh dear, that would never work for the museum. Do you have time on Thursday? I was getting together with the others, and we were planning to call you. We could come over. Anne's really the one you want going through your wardrobe, but I'll warn you, she can be ruthless."

"Ruthless?"

"Yes, she'll go through everything and tell you what to keep, what to donate and what to toss. Sage and Saoirse had already had a go at my closet, but they were amateurs compared to Anne. She's fairly imperious about it, but she's always right. Holmes worships the ground she walks on. Before I met Holmes, I tended to favor rather frumpy clothes. He kept encouraging me to buy things that better suited my body and my personality. He finally asked Anne for her help. She gutted my closet. I ended up with only about a third of what I had. I hate to admit it, but I'm so glad he did. The new things I have and the things I kept really make me feel better about myself. I look so much more polished and just feel more in tune with who I really am at my core. The funny part is that it translates to every other aspect of my life. Yes, my gorgeous, hunky husband thinks I'm sexier, but I look more like a successful businesswoman too—and I'm bringing in more money now than I ever have. I think the new look gave me a sense of confidence and pride. There are some situations I handle better because I feel like the clothing gives me a kind of armor."

Corinne smiled, picturing it. "Then, I am definitely signing up for the Anne Watson makeover."

"Oh good God, don't tell her that. She'll make you get a hair and makeup redo as well."

"I don't think that's a bad thing, but I don't know if you could do it in a day. I'd love it if all of you came. I'm hopeless where fashion is concerned."

"Nice thing about Anne is that she loves fashion, but she's also incredibly practical. What do you say we come by about eleven?"

"That would be great."

Corinne ended the call, feeling far more confident about having what she needed to start her new job and finally ready to turn in. She puttered around her flat, just thinking about getting ready for bed, when her mobile rang again. When she glanced at the caller ID, she laughed.

"Anne, I should have known you would be calling."

"Makeover? I'm in, but eleven won't do. Let's meet at the Savoy Grille at seven. My hairstylist doesn't usually open until ten, but he'll fit you in and his partner is a makeup artist. Then we'll go shopping, have lunch, and adjourn to your place over the restaurant where I will be decimating your closet." She laughed. "This is going to be so much fun."

Anne rang off without even giving her a chance to respond. Corinne shook her head. She had a feeling she was about to experience what Gabe referred to as Hurricane Anne. It really was the perfect way to end her day. She stripped out of her clothes, stretched and hopped into her old, merely adequate shower. She'd already started her countdown to having a better bathroom to luxuriate in.

~

Eddy watched her getting ready for bed. He kept himself from looking—that wasn't true; he looked, but he didn't stare—at Corinne's naked body as she stripped down. It wasn't that he didn't want to; she was the fodder for his masturbatory fantasies. He already used her laptop computer to keep tabs on her to ensure she was safe, but using it to spy on her just to see her voluptuous body without any clothes was a bridge too far. Watching Corinne, in or out of her clothes, was highly arousing and he spent enough time with a hard cock from unconsciously thinking about her. It just felt a bit creepy and stalkerish to intrude on her privacy to that extent.

Once she'd crawled into bed, though, he contentedly watched her settle down and fall asleep. He smiled. It was silly, but he found great comfort in watching over her while she slept. Here in the book, he didn't really need sleep. Holmes, Spense and Roark all agreed that had been something that had taken them aback—their need to rest. But all three agreed that sleeping with your beloved was almost as good as fucking her…

Almost.

CHAPTER 7

The next few days flew by. Each day, Corinne made time to slip by her new place to take at least one box with her. Some days she had enough time to unpack it and others she didn't, but each time she felt she was making progress. Rachel had been incredibly generous with the things she had left behind—beautiful antique pieces that weren't at all fussy and were functional in the extreme.

The furniture wasn't the only thing Rachel had been kind about. The price she had named for the flat was easily within Corinne's market and gave her enough cash to not only fund her makeover but to buy new bedding and towels for her flat. When Rachel had remodeled, she'd had the entire flat repainted a beautiful cream color that not only complemented the natural wood beams, floors and trim throughout the flat, but the painted and distressed kitchen cabinets and island. What had surprised and delighted Corinne was Rachel's use of natural soapstone for all the counters throughout the flat, with the exception of the counters in the walk-through closet, which were a gorgeous Brazilian red granite.

Anne called Thursday morning at six. "Black leggings, black or solid top and comfy shoes."

Corinne laughed. "Good morning to you too. I'm not coming to the Savoy without makeup."

"That's fine; they can remove it before your minifacial. Just pull your hair back. See you soon."

Anne ended the call before Corinne could respond. Without a doubt, Anne was used to being in command, which was why it seemed odd that she would ever be submissive. And yet, when Corinne saw her with Gabe, it was obvious who the dominant partner was. In fact, ever since she and Spense had talked last week, she'd had a chance to observe all four couples and could see how each was unique, but how special they all seemed. Maybe that lifestyle was worth considering if she found the right man.

Corinne snorted at her own foolishness. Man? Relationship? She barely had time to breathe; there was no way she could add a man into the mix.

She arrived at the Savoy just a few minutes before seven. It occurred to her that she rarely ventured into the hotel unless she was working. It was a beautiful and grand old building complex, considered to be one of the best luxury hotels in the world. As a member of the staff, she knew they prided themselves on top-notch accommodations and world-class service.

The hostess for the Savoy Grille greeted her and showed her to their table. "Anne and Sage are already here. Anne commandeered the best table for you guys. God, I wish I had half her style and confidence."

"You and me both. The girls are taking me out for a makeover today…"

"That would be so much fun. I can't wait to see what they do with your hair and makeup… not that you look bad…" the hostess stammered.

"I like to think of myself as a blank canvas," teased Corinne.

"Hey, sweetie," said Sage as Corinne took her seat.

It didn't take long before the quintet was completed by the arrival of Saoirse and Rachel.

"I just want you to know, Spense was not amused that I was leaving so early on his day off," quipped Saoirse. "But I reminded him we were helping Corinne."

"He isn't foolish enough to think that you won't be shopping as well, is he?" asked Anne, a sly smile lifting the corners of her mouth.

"Oh God, no. He's much smarter than that."

"Holmes told me to have fun and buy him something."

"Are we going to a men's store?" asked Corinne.

The other four women laughed, and Rachel placed her hand on Corinne's arm. "That's Holmes-speak for, 'Buy something so sexy I'll want to rip it off your body'."

Corinne looked around the table at her companions and decided she was in good hands for her makeover. Once they'd had breakfast, they adjourned to the hairstylist they all used where she had her makeup removed. Corinne was treated to a mini-facial before being handed over to the hairstylist, where she was given strict instructions to keep her eyes closed. Instead of being nerve-racking, she was finding that it added to the excitement and fun.

The stylist explained what he was doing—adding highlights, lowlights and lots of layering—but they wanted her to wait until both he and the makeup artist were finished before she took a gander at the new and improved Corinne Adler.

"You have such exquisite skin," said the makeup artist. "Instead of foundation, I'm just going to use tinted moisturizer, which has SPF protection and will even out your skin tone without being heavy."

He took Corinne through both skin care and makeup, and she realized it took less time than it normally took her. The hairstylist had also promised her easy, wash and wear hair. When they spun her around and asked her to open her eyes, Corinne was gobsmacked. Staring back at her was a woman she'd not only never seen before, but hadn't known existed. She felt gorgeous, feminine, powerful and most of all, herself. Six faces clustered around hers in the mirror, waiting anxiously.

"I remember reading that Michelangelo once said every stone has a sculpture within it, and it's up to the artist to reveal it. That's how I feel… like you guys revealed the me that was always there. It's amazing." She brought her hand up to touch her cheek and then ran her fingers through her barely curly hair.

"Mimosas all around," said Sage, breaking out champagne and orange juice.

While they each sipped their drinks, Corinne couldn't help looking at her reflection again and again. "I can't believe the difference you guys made. I just feel beautiful."

"That's the reaction every stylist wants to hear. And it should be super easy for you to maintain."

After purchasing both hair and skin products, Corinne and her personal fashion squad headed next to the foundation store.

When she handed Anne her sports bra, Anne held it up by one finger. "I'm going to assume this is the best you have?"

"I wish I could say no, but yes, that's the best of the lot." Anne rolled her eyes. "They're comfortable and work well."

"Sweetie, they call them a *sports* bra for a reason," said Sage, gently.

Within the hour, she had an array of new bras that she had to admit enhanced her figure. She'd been a bit shocked when she had to suggest panties, and all four women admitted that unless they were going to a club and it was a thong that matched their corset, they didn't bother. She bought one pair of matching panties for each bra but promised when they went out to dinner that night, she'd go without to experience the feel of it. That definitely intrigued her.

As they left the foundation store, Anne said, "Hmm... Anyone up for causing a little trouble?"

Saoirse started laughing. "Have you ever known this lot not to be? What do you have in mind?"

"I think our newest member needs a corset."

"Why do I need a corset?" asked Corinne.

"Because Anne wants to cause trouble, and you're the perfect foil," explained Rachel. "And for the record, I am absolutely in, but what makes you think Louis will relent?"

"Easy. We're going to play on the fact that he loves to make women feel beautiful and special. We'll tell him it's all part of her makeover. Besides, I don't think he'll be able to resist the idea of helping her find her first corset to introduce her to the lifestyle."

Sage laughed. "How can she find a Dom if she isn't properly dressed? And does he really want her to have to wear one of the ones they offer training subs at Baker Street? You really are evil, Anne."

"Evil, but persuasive."

Corinne couldn't help but get caught up in their fun and camaraderie. Besides, it would give her a chance to talk to them about their chosen lifestyle. Ever since the brief conversation with Spense, Corinne had been intrigued.

"I'm in," she said. "I've been trying to figure out how to broach the subject of your lifestyle and Baker Street. I mean, I know what Baker Street is; the Savoy has a lot of high-powered guests who are interested in it."

Saoirse nodded. "Spense said the two of you talked briefly, and he thought he might have given you food for thought. I think I can speak for all of us... Ask whatever you like. If someone feels uncomfortable answering, they won't."

"Let's see if we can persuade Louis to help us..." suggested Sage.

"I think if we can, we should promise to keep it to ourselves. If the other subs at the club find out we got him to bend his rules, he'll be inundated. And he really does believe that Doms should be involved," said Anne.

"I'm surprised to hear you say that," said Saoirse.

"Sweetie, true power isn't about who knows what you did. True power comes from being able to do it so that you get your own way. Think about it—wouldn't you love to surprise your significant other with a new corset now and again? If we pull this off, I'm going to get him to make me several to take with me when we immigrate. I talked to JJ, and she says there are some good custom corset makers on the East Coast, but the best one is Cable Car Corsets in San Francisco. It would be so much easier when I want a new one to just call Louis and have it sent."

Once they arrived at the Dark Garden, a custom corsetier, they had to wait before Louis would even deign to receive them.

"Anne, this is highly unusual," he admonished their leader.

"I know, Louis, but our friend Corinne is having a complete makeover. We bought her all-new underthings. She has on one of her new bras now. I won't show you the awful bandage thing she was using before. You'd have to put your eyes out, it's so ugly."

Louis grinned. It would seem even the crusty corset maker wasn't immune to Anne's charms.

"Besides," Anne continued, "if she's going to go to Baker Street, you'll want her to look her best to catch the eyes of the right Dom, won't you? And who, but you, could help her with that? Please, Louis, we all promise not to tell a soul. Don't we, ladies?"

They all agreed, and Louis shook his finger at her. "You are a mischievous minx and if I was half my age, I might challenge your Gabriel for you."

"Really? I'd never thought of you as a masochist," Anne teased.

"*Bien*. But I must have your word that what I'm about to do goes no further than the six of us."

"I'll get Spense to say he sponsored her. He works with Corinne and is extremely fond of her. In fact, Spense was the first person Corinne talked to about all this."

Anne not only persuaded Louis to make Corinne a beautiful brocade corset that complimented her coloring, but to make her a new one as well so she could surprise Gabe with it for his birthday.

When they left the Dark Garden, they stopped for lunch at one of the multitude of pubs in London's vintage shopping district. At breakfast, they had discussed what Corinne wanted, which was a mix of Rachel's very polished and professional look with Sage's slightly quirky one. While she loved Saoirse and Anne's more bohemian style, they all agreed that it might be a bit much for her work at the National Gallery, at least to start.

"Who will you be working for?" Rachel asked as she took a bite of her macaroni and cheese.

"Gloria Burton."

"Oh, you'll like her, and you can probably push a little on your style—maybe not the first day, but fairly quickly. Most of the time, Gloria likes to dress pretty avant-garde."

"Gloria said she knew you and had been to your place," said Corinne.

"Gloria is also a member of Baker Street," said Anne. When the others looked at her with dismay, she waved a hand in the air, dismissing their concern.

"What? It's not like we don't know Corinne, and she isn't going to go blabbing to everyone and his brother."

"Sometimes Anne forgets some people don't want their membership at a kink club to be public knowledge, so it's treated as confidential," soothed Rachel.

"I just don't get what the big deal is," carped Anne.

"Because you are a notorious exhibitionist," laughed Sage. "You wouldn't know discretion if it punched you in the face."

By the time lunch had ended, they had a game plan for the rest of the day. They stopped first at the bedding and bath store Corinne wanted to visit, and the proprietress arranged for her purchases there as well as her other purchases to be delivered later that afternoon to the flat over the Indian restaurant.

The rest of the afternoon was a whirlwind of shopping, trying on clothes and having Anne reject things. Corinne had to admit, Rachel was right. The dark-haired beauty understood fashion and what would look good on a woman's body. By the time they were done, Corinne had, even without the addition of whatever pieces Anne let her keep from her old wardrobe, enough clothes for two weeks at the museum without a repeat.

They arrived at Corinne's old flat just in time to accept the delivery, and between the five of them, getting everything upstairs was easily accomplished.

She wasn't sure when it had happened, but sometime during the day she had ceased to feel like an interloper and more like she had just joined the musketeers. She might be the fifth wheel, but she meant to be a damn good one.

"Here it is," Corinne said with a flourish as she opened the door.

The first indication that something had gone awry was the sound of Sage's gasp. Inside, it looked like a bomb had gone off in her flat. Immediately, Rachel got on the phone to Holmes, who asked them to return with their purchases to the Indian restaurant and wait.

CHAPTER 8

Corinne pushed past Sage and Rachel, running to the ornate blanket chest at the end of her bed. It lay open, and some of her bedding had been gone through, but she breathed a sigh of relief when she pulled up the false bottom and the cases containing her sword and her bow rested there undisturbed. Pulling the two cases from the chest, she replaced the lid on the trap door, she tossed the contents back in before standing up to rejoin her friends.

"I can't leave these here. They're too valuable."

"Remember to tell Holmes you went in there and took them," said Rachel.

"They aren't going to send a DSI for a petty theft break-and-enter."

"The Yard might not send anyone at all. But Holmes has friends in Forensics, and they'll come as a favor to him, and I suspect it'll be Roark with either Gabe or Spense who shows up," said Saoirse.

"Did we happen to mention that by becoming one of us—you do know you're part of our group now, right?—you just inherited four older brothers. Thankfully, the most obnoxious of the lot will be moving to America," quipped Anne.

It didn't take long for Roark and Gabe to show up, with one of Holmes' friends from the forensic unit not far behind. The women were instructed to stay downstairs in the restaurant while Gabe and Roark had a look around.

The man from Forensics didn't take long and stopped to tell them, "The only useable prints were yours, I suspect, but I'll double check that. I'm sorry I couldn't be of more help and that this happened to you."

"How did they get in?" asked Corinne.

"From the scratches on the deadbolt, my guess is they picked the lock. Do you think they took anything?"

"I don't know. Holmes asked us to come back down here and wait, so I haven't had a chance to take a look," answered Corinne, hoping the others might not mention her little foray into the flat.

After he left, Rachel said quietly, "We stick together. Unless it becomes apparent they need to know, we operate on the presumption that what they don't know can't hurt us." The others agreed immediately, a relief to Corinne as she needed to protect her aunt's gifts—the weapons—at all costs.

"Ladies," greeted Gabe as he approached them. "Everyone okay? Let's get all of you upstairs. Corinne, if you could go through your things and make a list of what might be missing, it would be helpful."

Roark had joined them; he and Gabe lugged the purchases the ladies had made back up the stairs. Corinne was worried that the break-in might cast a pall on their day, but that notion was soon disabused as Anne started going through her clothes—at first just those strewn around the room and then in the cupboard and drawers. Comments of 'hideous,' 'tragic,' and one 'oh my god," accompanied her thorough, ruthless sorting.

"If she's upsetting you, I'll make her stop," said Gabe in a quiet undertone to Corinne. "But it's helping her calm back down, and I understand you were going to have her go through your things any way…"

"It's fine, Gabe. I kind of thought Rachel might be exaggerating about how little Anne left her, but I'm beginning to think if I even keep a third of my old clothes, I'll be doing well."

"The only reason Rachel got to keep a third of hers was because Saoirse and Sage had done a preliminary sort," said Anne as she continued to decimate Corinne's wardrobe.

Gabe laughed. "My beautiful bride is quite the fashionista and really wants her friends to look fabulous, which by the way, your hair does."

"Thanks," Corinne said with a grin. "Until we came home and found this, I'd had the best day. It's weird, but it looks like all they took was my toaster, mobile charger, and Bluetooth speakers. Granted, they were nice, but kind of weird."

"I noticed that. Your laptop is still here; it doesn't even look like they touched your jewelry or anything else." He mused for a moment, hand on chin. "It almost looks like they were searching for a specific item or information, and it obviously wasn't on your computer."

"How do you know that?"

"The computer?" Gabe shrugged. "I searched the activity log. Looking for something in particular?" He gestured to the mess the thieves had made. "The way they dashed through things and what they left behind. So, what is it they were looking for?" He glanced over at Anne, who had made two distinct piles of clothing and was now hanging less than a quarter of Corinne's things back up. "Babe, what do you want to do with those clothes you have separated out?"

"The pile on the left can go downstairs into the rubbish. The other needs to be boxed up to take to charity. The handbags have got to go, except for this one," Anne said, holding up a vintage black Coach hobo bag. "And the shoes are almost as bad. A couple of the pairs of boots are okay, and I'll leave you two pairs of trainers, pumps and sandals. But when the budget allows, we're going to need to go shopping for shoes."

"Can you ladies box up Corinne's clothes and toiletries? Did I see new bedding?" Gabe asked. Corinne nodded. "Good. Both Roark and I brought our vehicles, and Holmes is going to pick up Spense on the way over. We're moving you into your new place tonight with what you'll need for the next few days. Saturday morning, we'll pick you up bright and early and come get the rest of your things."

"I don't think…" Corinne started to protest.

"Corinne, I think the rest of us would feel better if you didn't stay here. It's as Gabriel indicated," Roark said. "It's fairly obvious they were looking for something."

Corinne nodded. "The only piece of furniture that's mine is the blanket chest, and that's where I kept my two most valuable possessions."

"Do you think that's what they were looking for?"

"Probably. We can leave the chest until Saturday, but I want my weapons with me."

"You have a gun?" asked Gabe in a surprised voice.

Anne reached into Corinne's closet and pulled out the elegant, yet hefty, halberd and quarterstaff stored secretly there. "Based on these two, it isn't a gun she has in those cases," she said with a laugh.

Six pairs of eyes turned on her.

Corinne breathed out in a quiet huff. "No, it's not guns. It's an antique bow and sword that have been in my family for centuries. They were part of my inheritance from my aunt. She asked that I learn how to use them."

Instead of the alarm she expected, the others simply nodded, as if there was nothing strange about it. Perhaps hunting ghosts at the Savoy and their other activities made Corinne's secret seem normal to them.

"If you haven't found an instructor," offered Sage, "Steven Holcroft is one of the top fight masters in the world. I've used him as a resource on several books. I could arrange an introduction."

Corinne smiled. "He isn't one of the best, he is *the* best—just ask him."

Sage grinned. "So you've met."

"We have. Actually, he's a great teacher and his chauvinistic tendencies only show up once in a while."

Roark turned back to Corinne. "Does he know about your weapons?"

"Holcroft has seen the halberd and the quarterstaff. In fact, he helped me to acquire them. He knows I have a sword and a bow, but not a whole lot else."

Gabe nodded. "I'll make sure Holmes knows about that." The other four women had been gathering her things, and they had it all by the door, prepared to go. "If everyone's ready, let's get your weapons and head for your new place. If you want, we can either go out for food, or I can have Holmes and Spense bring us takeaway."

"If those are as valuable as I think they probably are, I'd have some kind of safe installed," said Rachel. "I found after I did the closet organization, I had two whole drawers that I really didn't need. I'll bet it would be easy enough to have them converted into a hidden safe."

Corinne brightened. "That's an excellent idea."

They took all the clothes Anne was letting her keep, as well as her toiletries, a few personal items and all they'd purchased earlier in the day and trucked them back down the stairs and into Gabe's SUV. Rachel, Saoirse and Corinne joined Roark and Sage in their vehicle while Anne rode with Gabe and all of Corinne's things.

By the time they arrived at Charing Cross, Holmes and Spense were waiting for them. The use of the lift made getting everything up to her flat much easier than schlepping them down from her old place had been. She didn't want to admit it, but she wasn't sorry Gabe and Roark had insisted on moving her into her new place this evening. She knew she'd sleep better in a safer flat, one that hadn't been broken into.

The next few hours felt more like a party than trying to get unpacked and settled into a new place. Saoirse and Sage shooed her and Rachel into the bath to get her toiletries unpacked; Anne took on closet organization. They broke down boxes and put packing paper into clean trash bags. There was a place right around the corner that took packing materials and redistributed them to those in need. By the time Spense and Gabe came back with pizza, Holmes had returned from a brief grocery run with just enough food staples to get her by.

As she looked around her new space, with everything in order and friends present, Corinne could feel the tension lessening. "I can't thank all of you enough. I have to say, at first I was a bit annoyed that Gabe just decided I was moving, but I don't think I would have been able to sleep in my old flat, so thank you, Gabe."

"My pleasure," he said, tilting his bottle toward her.

"Yes, he gets a great deal of pleasure from being bossy," teased Anne as everybody laughed.

"Says the woman who does the pleasuring," he rejoined.

Corinne admired the easy sexuality that seemed to flow between the various couples. The flat was spacious, but it would have been difficult to find adequate seating for eight other adults. But Saoirse and Anne were ensconced in their husbands' laps, Sage was snuggled up next to Roark and Rachel was seated on the floor between Holmes' legs with her head resting on his thigh.

"You have a curious look on your face," said Sage.

"I know that all of you have great marriages. I

would have to be an idiot not to know, but I don't think I really realized how great until now. You're all just so comfortable in your own skins and with each other. Almost makes me wish I had the time," replied Corinne, thoughtfully.

"You have a lot of demands on your time, that's for sure," said Gabe. "But if you want a bit of unsolicited advice, making time for someone special is more than worth the effort. And if you don't have time or interest in a twenty-four/seven relationship, you might want to think about becoming a member of Baker Street. There's something to be said, especially when you're crazy busy, about getting some help with structure and support."

"Not to mention getting your other needs seen to," added Anne. "If Gabe hadn't come bursting into my life the way he did, I might have taken some comfort and pleasure there. You do have to go through a training class, especially if you're not experienced, but that alone can teach you a lot about yourself."

"I'm going to think about it," said Corinne.

"If you decide you're interested, just let one of us know," said Sage.

When they'd finished eating and cleaned up the kitchen, Corinne saw her friends to the lift, then went back to her new flat, closed and locked the door and set the alarm system. She sighed in relief, feeling far more comfortable than she ever would have back in her old place.

Corinne decided to indulge that hedonistic part of her that she'd been catering to all day. While she let the large soaking tub in her bath fill with warm water, she entered her walk-in closet, amazed at the job Anne had done. Her new clothes went perfectly with the few remaining ones she had left, and they'd all been organized within an inch of their lives. Anne had deliberately left the two bottom drawers in the one dresser stack empty, and Corinne now carefully placed each of her weapons in one. Spence had promised to get her the name of the carpenter who could do the work of turning the drawers into a locked safe.

When the tub was filled, she shrugged out of her clothes, putting them in the hamper and then grabbed her electronic reader, intending to read while she soaked. She'd been encouraged to buy a lovely bath tray, specially designed to fit a slipper tub, and outfitted with a bookrest and a drink holder. Easing into the steamy scented water, she sighed. It had been a long time since she had indulged. The cast iron meant her water would stay hot longer than in a ceramic or plastic tub.

She opened up *Stack of Corpses*, one of the Clive Thomas novels that Sage had written. Corinne knew most women lusted after Roark, but some, like her, thought that some of the secondary characters were more interesting. Corinne's book boyfriend from the series was the black hat hacker, Eddy Chastain. The dark-haired, lean but muscular computer master had always intrigued her. Sage described him as having angular features, full lips and soulful brown eyes. To Corinne, his physical description was so much more intriguing than the run of the mill hunk-of-the-month. When she closed her eyes, she could picture Eddy with his luscious, silky hair and closely cropped beard or stubble. Even though not as physically intimidating as Roark or some of the others, Sage had taken great care to ensure that readers didn't see him as a typical geek or nerd and had described his cut chest, chiseled abs and those delicious, defined notches where his sculpted torso joined with strong legs.

Yep, the character of Eddy Chastain could step out of the pages of Sage's book anytime he wanted.

CHAPTER 9

Watching his friends spend the evening with Corinne had been frustrating and difficult. He was grateful that they had taken the time to get her set up in her new home. Not being able to figure out who had broken into her place was becoming something of an issue for him. He had a screenshot of the intruder, not a particularly good one, but certainly one that would help someone identify him as the perpetrator.

He needed to talk to Holmes. He sent a message to him and waited for his response.

Holmes: Eddy? What's up? Corinne is fine and we got her set up in her place in Charing Cross, but I suspect you already know that.

Eddy: I do. I'm sending you a screenshot of the guy. Your assumption that it wasn't random is right.

The guy was clearly looking for something. He only took the things he did to try and make it appear to be just a normal B-and-E.

Holmes:I figured. It might have fooled Corinne, but any kind of cop would have figured it out. Did you know about the weapons?

Eddy:I did. The bow is worth a mint. It was supposed to have been picked up at the Battle of Hastings. And the sword is priceless. According to her aunt, the sword is Galatine—one of the swords from King Arthur's knights.

Holmes:Like, Knights of the Round Table? Seriously?

Eddy:Yes, and from what I've been able to find out, she could be right.

Holmes:What the hell is Corinne Adler doing with an ancient bow and a priceless broadsword?

Eddy:Family heirlooms.

Holmes:That apparently she's able to use. According to Rachel, she's been training with some fight master.

Eddy:Steven Holcroft. Good at his craft. She's in the bath right now.

Holmes:You do know that's a bit creepy, right?

Eddy:I know. I try to keep it on a professional level, but sometimes I can't help myself and I steal a look. She's gorgeous, Holmes. I can't believe someone hasn't gobbled her up.

Holmes: Just in case you weren't listening, she's thinking about checking out Baker Street.

Eddy: You can't let her do that!

Holmes: I can't bloody well stop her. If you want a chance with Corinne, you're going to need to find a way through the Veil. And don't give me that bullshit about helping us. You can do that just as well from this side.

Eddy: You're probably right, but if I come out, there's no going back.

Holmes: I get that, but she's not making the trip to your side. And didn't you say it was beginning to feel like the boundaries around you were getting tighter and tighter?

Eddy: Yes. I talked with Saoirse. She feels like there's some kind of shift coming. She suspects that any and all other portals are being sucked out of existence to feed something else that's bigger and stronger.

Holmes: Then you need to come. You're an integral part of the team and if we lose you, we could be screwed.

Eddy: Nice of you to say…

Holmes: Truth. We'd have been hard pressed to deal alone with what happened to Sage, Rachel, Anne or Saoirse. Your research was invaluable in all those cases. You can access the dark web from this side of the Veil…

Eddy: Not nearly as easily.

Holmes: Easy isn't always the best reason to do or not do something. Think about it. I'd hate to see you wait until it's too late.

Eddy: But there's so much I'd have to do…

Holmes: No, you don't. If you don't come through the Veil with all your character's identity, bank accounts, etc., we know a master forger who can set you up. You can stay at the townhouse with Rachel and me. Hell, we've got a gatehouse. We can remodel it and set it up with everything you need. Just think about it.

Eddy: I will. Give Rachel a kiss from me.

Holmes: You kiss your own girl and keep your full, sensual French lips—Sage's description not mine—away from my wife.

Eddy: Will do. I'll keep an eye on Corinne and see what I can find out from here about the guy who broke in.

Holmes: Good man. I'll see what we can do on our end. Take care.

Screen Blips Off

Eddy spent the next several hours chasing down leads and bits of information regarding Corinne's family, legends about Big Ben and the Landseer lions, and the guy who'd broken into her old place over the Indian restaurant. When he finally came up for air, he was sure that the space he had always occupied was definitely smaller. Here or there things were missing—a piece of furniture, a picture on the wall. The room still seemed well appointed, just things he knew had once been there were now gone. Saoirse and Holmes were right. The time had come to either get out or face the very real possibility that he would be trapped forever.

Before he'd become involved with her, Eddy had considered allowing his sentience to slip away and fade back into the story, forgetting his friends and the life he'd never had. Life had been simpler before he'd become aware. That was the real crux—he hadn't known before, and now he did.

Corinne had changed all that. Now he longed for the woman who lay nestled in her new bed. She had become the driving force to break free. There rested the real question—did he want Corinne enough to pierce the Veil, even if he might never win her? Was he willing to risk everything for that one chance to claim her as his own?

As with most things in computer code, the old adage of *garbage in/garbage out* applied. More than that, though, it was essential to find the correct solution. And to do that, you had to ask the right question. Once he framed the real question—was Corinne worth it?—he had his answer. He had no other choice. Corinne was worth everything.

The following morning, he allowed himself the luxury of watching her get up and wander around her new apartment in the nude. He wondered if her friends had any idea that when alone, she had a preference for being naked. It certainly wasn't something he wanted to see change. When she left her new flat to head to the market, he enjoyed seeing her in tight denim leggings, an over-sized cable-knit sweater in light blue and a pair of navy-blue boots. Thankfully, the sweater hung low enough to cover the way the leggings showed off her spectacular ass.

Roark had pierced the Veil when Sage's life was in imminent danger. Eddy didn't plan to wait for that to happen. It wasn't so much what he'd found in his latest round of research that bothered him; he was more concerned about what he *hadn't* been able to learn.

Holmes and Spense had somehow tumbled through the Veil and ended up on the other side without much say in the matter. Eddy planned to pierce the Veil and enter on his own terms, but to do that he would need Saoirse's help.

Eddy:Saoirse?

Saoirse:I'm here. Have you figured out a way through?

Eddy:How'd you know?

Saoirse:Holmes. He thought you might be on the verge, and I might be able to help, so he asked me to keep my laptop or phone close so you could reach me.

Eddy: Know any ways to open or strengthen a portal?

Saoirse: A portal into another dimension? That's beyond my scope and training, and I'm not about to experiment with your life.

Eddy: What if I could open, not so much a portal, but a little hole in the Veil. I have no corporeal form—well, not really. Sometimes I feel all too corporeal.

Saoirse: I don't think I'll ask which part or what causes that reaction or rather who.

Eddy: Not going there. But there's a ring of standing stones located in a cavern in Cornwall.

Saoirse: Carter's Wheel. As far as I know, it's the only formation of its kind. Kind of blows all the theories about circles of standing stones being some kind of calendar or astrological observatory. I know where it is; I have friends in that part of the country and even know the family that owns the land. Why?

Eddy: I think I can punch a hole in the Veil there without garnering too much attention. If I can, you could help me stabilize it and I should gain some kind of mass or form as I leave this side of the Veil. Once I do, I should be able to slip through and then we can let it close up. Once I'm on the other side—your side—I should be just like the rest of you, and you can give me a lift back to London.

Saoirse: Again, you're asking me to play out of my league. What happens if you don't materialize, and the doorway shuts down? Do you just cease to exist?

Eddy:I don't know. Probably. But you need to know, I'm not sure that won't happen if I don't try. I've been monitoring my space. It's getting smaller. I think you were right about some big bad trying to come through somewhere else and drawing energy to facilitate its exit. If I don't get out now, I never will. How long will it take you to get there?

Saoirse:Five to six hours; seven to be safe.

Eddy:I need your help, Saoirse. Do you think you and Spense can meet me there?

Saoirse:What makes you think I need Spense?

Eddy:I think if you don't bring him with you, you won't sit for a week when he gets through with you.

Saoirse:You know, my life was a lot easier when I was just a simple Irish witch making poultices and compounded medicines to order.

Eddy:But not nearly as much fun. And you know he adores you.

Saoirse:I do. So, it's eight in the morning here. Seven hours would make it three in the afternoon, which would work. Holding something open takes a massive amount of strength of masculine energies— fire and wind. Both are more prevalent during the day.

Eddy:Three it is. I'll reach out when I'm ready to ensure you are too.

Saoirse:You sure you're willing to risk it? I'm

telling you, it isn't as easy as Roark, Holmes and Spense think.

Eddy: But they didn't have a beautiful Irish witch on their side. And I don't think I have a choice. I either take this chance to come through, or I'll just blip out of existence. I can't decide which would be worse—to remain sentient if that happened or just disappear altogether.

Saoirse: I don't like either of those options, so we'll see you at Carter's Wheel.

Eddy: Thanks, Saoirse.

Screen Blips Off

Eddy spent the rest of the day trying to put in as many back doors to different places on the dark web as he could. He planned to try and enter the real world with his computer, but he'd set a self-destruct time on it for eight hours. If he got through the Veil, he'd have plenty of time to turn it off. If not, there would be nothing left behind for anyone to follow or use against his friends.

Six hours in, Eddy looked around for the markings he'd left at the corners of his little world. He couldn't see them. For the past several hours, he'd felt as if something were trying to reach him in his safe haven. He could almost feel something cold and evil grasping at the tendrils of his existence. The parameters of his world were definitely diminishing, and they were doing so at an increasingly rapid pace. Saoirse had originally said, five to six hours. Given the increasing rate of shrinkage, he decided to reach out.

Eddy:Saoirse?

Saoirse:We're here. We made good time. Are we still on for three?

Eddy:No. I've been monitoring my space. It's getting smaller and smaller. It was week-by-week, then day-by-day, then hour-by-hour. I'm not sure I can wait that long.

Saoirse:Spense has just closed off the cavern with a ring of salt, and he's spreading it all around the outside of the wheel. Give me a couple of minutes, and he should be done. When I cast my spell, he'll enter 'now' and hit send. Come then and come hard. If you're right and something wants to stop you, we'll only have one shot at this.

Eddy:Understood. Whatever happens, I wouldn't have missed knowing any of you for the world.

Saoirse:We can do this. You need to be on this side. You're right about something coming, and I think Corinne may be at the heart of it.

Eddy waited, focusing his laser light source on a space he had pinpointed. He could just barely make out a perceptible difference in density and light on the other side.

Saoirse:Now!

Eddy stepped back and ran at the expanding

opening in the Veil, hitting it with his shoulder, wedging it in and forcing his way through.

"Come on, Eddy!"

"We can see you!"

"You've got this buddy!"

"Push, Eddy!"

He could hear their distinct voices—Roark, Spense, Gabe and Sage. His friends had come to welcome him into their world. He struggled harder. Breathing was difficult, but his lungs were forcing him to gulp for air. He felt something wrap its gnarly fingers around his ankle, but he kicked it off with his other foot.

Eddy tossed his laptop the rest of the way through the opening, then grasped the edges and pulled with all his might. His muscles stretched and warmed as they formed, their corporeal version seeming to come on-line and threatening to collapse until they found a strength of their own. He dragged himself forward, feeling the Veil collapsing in all around him. It sucked at his mass and at his energy. His fingers started to lose their grip.

No! He couldn't fail. He had to get through.

Just as all his muscles spasmed, his hands opened without warning—and whatever it was that had kept him on the side of the Veil he'd started on cackled and began to draw him back through. As the last of his strength deserted him, four strong hands grasped him from under the shoulders, using him as the tether in a deadly game of see-saw.

"Don't give up, Eddy. We've got you!" shouted Gabe.

But the beast on the other end refused to yield. Eddy twisted and smashed his foot against it just as Gabe and Roark pulled... And he slipped through the opening, landing on the cold, hard ground of the cavern in a heap with his friends.

CHAPTER 10

*E*ddy pushed up, his fingers flexing into the hard-packed earth. The air was cold, a frigid wind coming from the Atlantic Ocean, whistling through the tunnel that led back to where Carter's Wheel stood.

"I made it," he said, somewhat astonished.

"And fully clothed. Damn. If I'd known that, I'd have stayed at home," teased Sage.

"That is quite enough out of you," said Roark, getting to his feet, dusting himself off and extending a hand to Eddy. "It's good to see you."

"For a minute there, I wasn't sure we were going to get you through," said Gabe.

Taking Roark's hand, Eddy stood on terra firma for the first time. "If whatever had a hold of me on the other side had its way, you wouldn't have. Did anybody see my laptop?"

"I picked it up, and I've got it under my coat," answered Sage.

"Let me have it. I need to cancel the self-destruct."

"You sent a bomb through the veil?" asked Spense, eyebrows shooting up in alarm.

"Of course not. It would have just fried the motherboard and destroyed everything it contained, including the links and back doors I've built for myself. I had it set so that if I didn't make it, all the info I've got on there couldn't be used against any of you." Sage handed him the laptop, and he quickly entered the command code to stop the countdown.

Then he took a deep breath and looked around, more relaxed. "Damn, it's good to see all of you. I only thought it would be Spense and Saoirse."

"And let them have all the fun without us?" asked Gabe with a smile. "Rachel had a tour. I left Anne with Corinne. Apparently, your girl has atrocious taste in footwear."

"She isn't my girl," Eddy said defensively. When all of them simply stared at him, he clarified. "*Yet*." He grinned. "I have to say, what I've seen of the things the girls bought on their shopping spree, has been wonderful. The best part is, she seems to love all of it… and feeling like she's finally been really accepted by all of you."

"We never meant to make her feel left out," started Sage.

"It was never you," Eddy reassured her. "Corinne just got caught up in her own life. It has been so busy and hectic for her, but finishing her doctorate, getting the job with the National Gallery, and buying Rachel's flat—all of that seems to have settled her in a good way. I think she's ready to start having a real life instead of just existing."

"Hmm… sounds like somebody else we know," said Roark.

Eddy grinned at him sheepishly. "I know… pot, meet kettle."

"I think it's great you're here, and I am all in favor of you and Corinne as a couple," said Saoirse.

"In case you missed it, there's a 'but' coming…" said Spense, wrapping his arm around his wife.

"But you need to remember that while you know her, she knows nothing of you." Turning to Sage, she said, "Are you checking?"

"Checking what?" said Eddy.

"The Clive Thomas books," answered Sage distractedly, paging through her works on her phone's book app. "Damn. You have been replaced by a German nerd named Elias, who is truly a geek. That is so weird."

"And the rest of us stepping out of the pages of your manuscript and being replaced by new characters wasn't?" asked Spense.

"Point taken," laughed Sage.

"I hate to be a killjoy, but if we're going to get

back to London at a reasonable hour, we need to get moving," said Gabe.

"There's a great little pub near here. We can grab a quick bite to eat and get on the road. We'd be back before eleven," offered Saoirse.

"I'll give Anne a call and let her know Eddy's here safe and sound, and that we'll be on our way after we grab some food."

They made their way in two SUVs to the pub, where they decided to eat family-style so Eddy could taste everything. The food was delicious, the beer too, and he marveled over the fact that he'd never realized how... *pale* in comparison, he supposed you could say... his meals inside the book had been.

"By the way, Anne said we're all to head to Corinne's where they'll have food," said Gabe. "I think we're going to get our marching orders for tomorrow," he chuckled.

"What's happening tomorrow?" asked Eddy.

"We're picking up the rest of Corinne's things from her old flat..."

"Sage and I talked," added Saoirse. "Spense was pretty clear that none of you felt comfortable with any of us staying behind to clean up..." She laid her hand on Holmes' arm to forestall an argument. "...so we hired a cleaning agency to come and do a final cleanup."

"How do you guys plan to explain me?" asked Eddy as they left the pub and split off into the two

SUVs: Eddy, Roark and Sage in one; Spense, Saoirse and Gabe in the other. The latter would swing by and pick up Rachel before joining them in Charing Cross.

"I'll just say you've been one of my research sources and that I asked you to come help with the move," explained Sage. "I know all kinds of people who do all kinds of things. Check to see if you came through with your identification and personal resources intact like Spense, Roark and Holmes did. If not, we know a master forger. She helped to set up Anne's identity. But the others came through with all the stuff from their backstory, so you probably did too."

Eddy opened his laptop and began laughing. "That is weird. I'm glad Sage made me a reclusive hacker with a lucrative business. And I'm really no longer in the books?"

"I'm afraid not. Like Roark, Holmes and Spense, you've been replaced by some new guy. He isn't nearly as interesting or endearing as you. The weird thing is that no one else knows that the characters were ever different. Of course we told Gabe, Anne, Rachel and Saoirse, but they wouldn't have known if we hadn't told them," explained Sage.

"Do you think Corinne will be disappointed in me?" he asked Sage.

"Not at all. At least I described you as a hunk. Poor Spense. I'm so glad he didn't come through the Veil looking like I described him. The only thing that remained of his physical description was the scar. I think you should know, Eddy is Corinne's favorite character."

"Sage, that's enough" warned Roark. "You are not to play matchmaker."

Eddy laughed. "Don't listen to him, Sage—matchmake all you want."

"Do not encourage her."

"Oh hush," teased Sage. "I do think you should know she's become increasingly interested in the D/s lifestyle and is thinking about visiting Baker Street. I know that JJ Fitzwallace is planning a going-away party for Gabe and Anne. I'm sure she's going to attend."

"You don't know the half of it," Eddy shared. "She's been doing a ton of research online about the lifestyle."

"Okay, you need to stop doing that," said Sage, shaking her head.

"Doing what?"

"Monitoring all her activities. It's beginning to border on creepy."

"I understand what you're saying, and actually I don't disagree. But there's something going on with her; something she's keeping to herself. And I'm not the only one watching."

"What do you mean?" asked Roark, catching Eddy's eye in the rearview mirror. "And by the way, pet, I used to do the same thing when I was on the other side of the Veil. I kept a close eye on you and monitored all of your communications."

"Yes. Roark was a lot worse than I was. But good thing he was—or none of us would be here, and you'd be dead."

"Okay, but it stops now. Roark doesn't do that anymore—well, not much anyway."

"What do you think is going on with Corinne?" asked Roark.

"I'm not sure. I know you know about the weapons and her training. But there's a group called the Order of the Seven Maidens…"

"That sounds familiar," said Sage.

Eddy nodded. "It should. You did some research on them, but when you ran into a brick wall, you moved on… I didn't. They've been around since before England was England. It seems to have been a group of nuns who were violated and then left to die while their convent burned all around them."

"Vikings?"

"Most likely, but records and even stories from that time are confusing and conflicting. The women survived, but because they didn't choose to kill themselves before or after it happened, the church disowned and disavowed them."

"That's terrible," said Sage.

"It is. I had to dig to get to the heart of the matter. Instead of slinking away never to be heard from again, the women banded together and rebuilt their home. Eventually they built a self-sustaining community and produced honey, mead and ale. They also had a successful farm and bakery. They taught themselves to fight and tended to the sick and needy in their surrounding area. In short, they gave a happy middle finger to the church and to the male patriarchy."

"I'm surprised the patriarchy allowed that to happen."

"I think everyone involved felt guilty about what happened to them and how they were treated. They paid their taxes peacefully, and so the monarchies just ignored them. In the end, the people around them supported them and the order became wealthy, and I mean really wealthy. They've made some really smart and strategic financial moves over the centuries…"

"This is all fascinating," said Roark, "but what does it have to do with Corinne?"

Eddy smiled, leaning in eagerly to discuss the details. "This is where it gets truly interesting. You know about the weapons, right? One of the founding members of the Order was an ancestor of Corinne's, who was said to have descended along the female line from Merlin. She took up the sword and became a protector of the innocent. She had a daughter to whom she passed on both her calling and her weapons, a tradition that has continued to this day. The Order has supported each successive woman.

Corinne's aunt passed them on to her when she knew she was dying. Super cool, right?"

Roark shook his head. "Badly misguided is more like it. Why didn't one of these women get married and pass it down to her son? Please, pet, no rousing renditions of *I Am Woman*. Given the time in which this all started, it would make the most sense."

Ignoring her husband, Sage asked, "Did these women live a monastic life? I know Corinne said her aunt never married."

"Some did and some didn't. Interestingly, none of those to whom the weapons were given ever bore a son."

"So, a strong female line," said Sage, grabbing her tablet and making notes. "Does Corinne know any of this?"

"I don't think so. I mean, she knows about the weapons, and her aunt tried to impress upon her that she had a duty. But she was shocked when suddenly the Order started making regular deposits into her account. She doesn't know it's them or what it's for. In fact, she has a separate savings account that she transfers the money to each month. But that's not even the best part…"

Sage turned in her seat so she could see Eddy in the back. "Tell me."

"Did you know that some believe Big Ben was built over a portal into another dimension?"

"Like the Veil?" asked Roark.

"Exactly, but it isn't the nether world behind the Veil or the Void where Anne existed. It's a kind of demon dimension. They tried having solid clock faces for Big Ben, but the pieces kept shattering. Finally, they installed the faces with different-sized parts so they could carry them up and piece them back together. Legend has it if Big Ben…"

"Chimes thirteen times," interrupted Sage, "that England will fall."

"No that's the ravens at the Tower. With Big Ben, the Landseer lions are supposed to come to life. Some say to devour the city; others say to protect it. Since Big Ben was built, an Adler has lived in London and is supposed to lead the lions to fight the evil."

"Good God, you don't really believe that, do you?" scoffed Roark.

"Why not?" Gabe shrugged. "You, Spense, Holmes and I once only existed in a book. Anne was beheaded and refused to go into the Light until she could figure out a way to escape. And Saoirse not only called down the banshees to deal with Jack the Ripper, but also solved the murder of five little girls from the time of Queen Victoria."

Sage snorted in delight. "The funny part is, if someone pitched any of those to me as a possible plot for a novel, I'd tell them they were too far-fetched."

CHAPTER 11

Corinne had spent the day with Anne—shopping for shoes, having lunch, getting a mani/pedi and just walking her new neighborhood. They had a wonderful time, with perfect weather and lots of laughter to make the day speed by.

As they settled back into the two comfy armchairs at the Charing Cross flat, Anne said, "I'm really sorry I didn't get to know you better before now. I think we could have had all kinds of wicked fun, don't you?"

"I do. I just had such a crazy schedule and then when I think about it, you haven't been part of the picture for very long."

Anne laughed. "I've been around far longer than you might imagine."

"Can I ask you something?"

"Of course."

Corinne took a deep breath, and leaned toward

the other woman. "How did you know? With Gabe, I mean? I was surprised that you showed up with Saoirse and then, bam, the two of you were involved."

Anne nodded. "I'm sure it must have seemed odd and incredibly fast. I wish I had some great answer for you, but I don't. I think I was in love with Gabe even before I met him. It was like I knew the only other significant relationship in my life had been shit, and he was the antithesis of that. I got lucky that he knew himself well enough and believed in us that he made it happen."

"What do you mean?"

"I was so afraid to love him—so afraid to listen to my heart. Gabe was strong enough and brave enough that he was willing to risk everything to have me," said Anne, kicking off her shoes and curling her legs up underneath herself.

"He was always so busy. It seemed like the only intimacy he had, besides his close friendships with Spense, Roark and Holmes, was at Baker Street, and then only because he could control the time involved," said Corinne, sipping her coffee.

"Yes, Gabriel does like to be in control," Anne agreed with a smile, "but not for control's sake. I think exerting control is his way of finding peace. That he can do it in service to a woman's needs makes it just that much better for him."

Corinne shook her head just thinking about it all.

"None of you ever struck me as submissive until I started reading some of the sites Spense recommended."

"I know exactly what you mean. I rebelled at the idea of being submissive. I thought it meant I would have no power, no choices, no way to get what I needed. But I was so wrong. For me, Gabe provides a peaceful place I can exist without a lot of burdens on me. Before I met him, I was told I had to think of everyone else… that it was up to me to ensure everyone around me was happy. The fact that I was suffocating and that I had nothing for myself wasn't important. When I met Gabe, I wanted it to be all about me. He indulged me while also showing me that what I really wanted was a partnership where both people's needs are met."

"That does sound appealing," Corinne said. She glanced out the window, loving the view of London she now had, and it made her wonder something else. "So, do you want to move to America?"

"Interesting question. The answer is yes and no. I love our life here in England. Until I met all of you, I'd never had any close friends. Part of the responsibility for that rests on me and I know that, but that being the case, I cherish the friendships I have now—present company included. But I have some truly horrible memories of London, and Gabe believes that putting some distance between us and the city will help."

"But a whole ocean?"

"In for a penny; in for a pound," said Anne with a gentle shrug. "The fact is, he also made a commitment to the men in his old unit that they would come together and form a company that helps others. Part of our move to the Outer Banks is to honor that commitment. To be completely candid, I will follow Gabe wherever he wants or needs to go. As long as I am with him, I am home. He means everything to me."

The afternoon was gone, and night was coming on. Corinne's rumbling stomach reminded her that dinner time was approaching. She smiled at Anne. "I thought we could order Chinese and have it delivered. If the others haven't arrived by the time it comes, we can just reheat it when they get here. It cracks me up that with all this talk about control, Gabe seems perfectly content to let you be in charge of my move. By the way, have I thanked you for that?"

"You have indeed. I actually enjoy it. I like being organized. Gabe can be very organized, but it isn't something he enjoys so he just lets me do it. I think part of D/s is learning to play to each other's strengths. I can be a truly nasty bitch and then I feel terrible about it, so Gabe just nips it in the bud."

"Sage said they might have a friend of hers with them to help them get the move done quicker. He wanted to come up to London and he offered to help."

"Gabe said she uses Eddy as an expert when she's referencing anything that's computer or technology related."

They spent the remainder of their time just chatting and going through Corinne's closet, with Anne showing her different ways to wear and combine things they'd bought. Sooner than she expected, the security buzzer went off, indicating there was someone on the street wanting to get in. Corinne could see the others all standing on the street waiting to be allowed to enter.

"Why didn't they just come in?" asked Corinne.

"I thought you needed to let them."

"I suppose technically, but Rachel still has a key. I need to remember to ask her if she'd mind keeping it so that I have a backup if I lock myself out."

"Probably just trying to be respectful of your space."

"Probably. They made good time."

Corinne opened the door to allow everyone to enter the flat. The guys had the Chinese food with them, apparently having intercepted the delivery guy. As soon as the last member of the group, the new guy, Eddy, closed the door behind them all, Corinne sucked in a breath and had to steady herself. It was all she could do not to drool. He was gorgeous, but not in an overdone or feminine way. He was tall, angular and dark—eyes, hair and stubble. He wore casual linen trousers and a cashmere sweater that seemed molded to his muscled body—not tight, but as if it had been made specifically to drape and cling in all the right spots.

"Welcome," she said, feeling stupid for not knowing what else to say.

Sage turned and smiled brightly. "Corinne Adler, I'd like you to meet my friend, Eddy Chastain."

Corinne laughed until she realized Sage wasn't joking. *Eddy Chastain? Had Sage just introduced this man—who was the spitting image of the hacker character in Sage's books—to her with the character's actual name?*

"It is a pleasure to make your acquaintance," he said in a deep voice, which had a distinct, but soft French accent.

Eddy or Edouard Chastain in the books is French as well. This has to be some kind of joke.

"Okay, Sage, you got me. I'm afraid Sage knows that unlike most of her readers, my favorite character isn't Clive Thomas, but her mysterious black-hat hacker."

"You like Elias?" asked Sage.

"No, silly, not Elias. Eddy… Eddy Chastain."

The entire group exchanged furtive glances.

"You must not be as devoted a reader as you say. Elias Wagner is my hacker character. Granted I based his abilities on Eddy's, but as you can see, Eddy isn't a character. You must have just confused the two."

Corinne was certain she was wrong, but it seemed important to Sage that she accept her explanation, so for now she would do so. She enjoyed herself, chatting with everyone and getting to know just a little about the handsome Eddy through casual conversation.

After eating, visiting and getting their marching orders for the next day from Anne, her friends dispersed, and Corinne got ready for bed. As she crawled under the covers and plumped her pillows behind her, she picked up her electronic reader and searched for the name *Eddy*. When nothing appeared, she searched for Edouard and then Chastain with the same results. With equal parts of confusion, curiosity and concern, she searched for Elias and found the book riddled with his name. She switched to another Clive Thomas novel and then another and then another until she had searched each and every one of them—all with the same results. Eddy Chastain had been replaced with Elias Wagner, and what's more, Elias Wagner was a blond, reedy-looking, waif-like character.

What the hell was going on?

Corinne went online and bought another copy of one of Sage's novels, the one where Eddy/Elias played a prominent part in the story. Again, no mention of Eddy and lots of appearances by Elias. Knowing one of the girls on the front desk at the hotel was on duty, she called.

"Hey, Corinne. What's up?"

"I haven't unpacked my electronic reader, and I

was trying to remember the name of Sage's hacker…"

"You mean Elias? It's funny how Clive and the DSI are so hunky, and the head concierge and the hacker are so unappealing."

Corinne tried to hide her surprise, keeping her voice calm. "Yeah, I guess she didn't want fans demanding they get their own storylines as well."

"Probably. Is that all you wanted?"

"Yeah. You know how it is when something gets stuck in your brain."

"Oh, I know. It can keep you up all night."

"Thanks. Talk to you later."

Corinne hung up just as the security buzzer went off. She looked in the view screen of the security system, only to see Eddy looking up at her. Corinne punched the entry button. Time to get to the bottom of this.

∾

His friends may have fooled themselves into believing that they had bamboozled Corinne, but Eddy knew better. She was a cool customer. She'd allowed them to believe she was buying their story, but Eddy knew her expressions and body language far better than they did. She hadn't accepted Sage's explanation. If she was running true to form, in the time it took him to go with Holmes and Rachel, slip out of their townhouse and get back to Corinne, she'd have checked all of the Clive Thomas novels. She'd also probably called one of the people she knew from the hotel who was also a fan of Sage's novels to doublecheck with her.

Eddy didn't want her to be concerned or to think her friends were lying to her. If whatever was coming was as bad as he and Saoirse thought, and if Corinne was going to be in the fight, she'd need to trust them and vice versa.

She was waiting in the open doorway when he opened the lift's iron doors. She didn't say a word, just waved him into her flat before following him in and closing the door behind her.

"Want to tell me what that was all about?" she asked in a neutral tone.

"You're angry. Don't be."

"I haven't known you long enough for you to get to tell me how I feel."

He held up his hands. "I would never try to do that. I was only trying to say that I understand you are most likely feeling hurt and angry that your friends tried to lie to you. If I were in your shoes, I would feel the same way. For what it's worth, they didn't expect you to know, and they feel badly. I don't think you should question the depth of their friendship based on a wrong choice. To be fair, I'm sure they felt they were protecting me." Eddy went to stand by the Chesterfield loveseat. "I would appreciate if you would sit down with me and allow me to explain."

"And if I won't?"

"I will leave and let our friends know you are angry, and they must tell you the truth."

"Just like that?"

Eddy nodded. "Just like that."

"Why did they feel they had to lie to me?"

"Because they were afraid you wouldn't understand."

"How could they not trust me?"

"It isn't as easy as that, n'est-ce pas? After all, there are things you don't trust them with."

"Like what?"

"Like, your sword is Galatine, the shadow sword of Excalibur. Like, your aunt was the last Sentinel of the Portal and when she died, she passed the responsibility on to you... Shall I go on, or would you like to come and sit with me?"

"Who *are* you?" Corinne breathed.

Eddy smirked at her. "I am exactly who you think I am. I am Eddy Chastain, and I began life in the pages of a Sage Mathews novel."

CHAPTER 12

Corinne felt as though her knees might buckle. Eddy—could that really be his name?—took her hand and held it until she sat down with him on the loveseat. She looked down at his hand, feeling its warmth and the smooth texture of his skin. They were artistic hands with long fingers. She imagined they could fly across a keyboard in pursuit of information he wanted… or reach up into a woman's pussy to provide her with an inordinate amount of pleasure.

Where had that thought come from? The answer was obvious. If he was who he said he was, she'd had a thing for him for a long time. His character in the book was highly intelligent, a genius hacker and one who spent a lot of time doing the right thing. More than once, it had been Eddy's brilliance that had saved Sage's hero.

"How? Why?" she asked, trying to grasp it all.

"To tell you the truth, we aren't sure."

"*We* being you and Sage?"

"*Non. We* being Roark, Holmes, Spense and now me."

"I don't understand…"

"More than a year ago, all four of us were characters in a series of books Sage wrote about a character named Roark Samuels, a British spy who became a well-heeled private investigator with a penchant for spanking and fucking a succession of heroines…"

"No, those are the Clive Thomas novels."

Eddy shook his head, rubbing his thumb along the back of her hand. Corinne found it soothing and mesmerizing at the same time, much like the sound of his voice.

"*Non.* Clive Thomas now, but they started as Roark Samuels."

"So, did she pull the novels down and change the name when she met Roark?" she asked, trying to make sense of what he was saying.

"*Non.* When Roark pierced the Veil between this dimension and that of her books, Roark's character was somehow replaced. That's only one of the things we don't fully understand. As far as you and the rest of the world knows, the protagonist of those stories has always been Clive Thomas. The same is true of the DSI character and the Savoy's head concierge…"

"No, Spense hired me. I remember my interview…"

"Exactly," Eddy insisted. "That's what none of us has been able to figure out. And we also have no idea how Spense or Holmes got here. Holmes became sentient shortly after Roark, and then me, and then Spense. We spent some time trapped inside the manuscripts, but then one day I looked up to see Holmes and Spense had been transferred to the real world and their characters were replaced with new ones. The funny part about Spense was he didn't look at all how Sage had described him."

Corinne gave him a slight smile. While she didn't want to reveal her crush, she couldn't deny she liked his handsome features. "You look exactly like Eddy… the Eddy in the book."

Eddy laughed, looking down at his hands, his clothes. "Yes, thankfully! Anyway, we have no explanation for how Holmes and Spense got here and why they arrived about a week before Roark. All we really know is that they all ended up here with everyone believing they'd always been here, backstories intact, and that new characters had been substituted. It's strange."

"What about you, though? The other night in the bath, I was reading, and you were there as Eddy. Now, you are nowhere to be found in the books, and you've been replaced by Elias."

With a shrug, Eddy replied, "I remained behind because I thought I could be of the most use to my friends by staying in the book. But I began to believe the world on the other side and my self-awareness were collapsing. Things were closing in on me. Combined with my inability to trace some information and Saoirse's intuition about something bad coming, we made a plan for me to escape."

"To Cornwall?"

"To Carter's Wheel. A place of old and powerful magick. A private place where if anything went wrong, it could be contained and dealt with."

She snapped her fingers. "So just like that, poof, you're here?"

"No, it was a combination of drawing on the power of the wheel, Saoirse's incantations and a focused laser beam of energy that allowed me to squeeze through." He shook his head, as if remembering his escape. "Trust me, the other side was none too happy about it."

A shiver ran down her spine. "What do you mean?"

"Saoirse and I have been both sensing a shift in power behind the Veil, as if something is causing it to concentrate in a central space, drawing strength from other openings. As I was coming through the gateway we created, something grabbed my ankle and tried to anchor me in the Veil. If it weren't for Roark and Gabe, I'm not sure I would have made it."

"Does Anne know? Does Gabe? What about Rachel? What about Sage?"

"Sage and Rachel were the first to know," he

assured her. "I think Sage is probably the one who could most identify with how you're feeling. She, too, remembered the originals—she created them. Rachel knew when the spirit of Jack the Ripper, or at least the man who murdered Mary Kelly, attached himself to Rachel and she found Holmes and Roark when the thing was terrorizing her. When they fell in love, Holmes had no choice but to tell her."

Corinne drew back, dismayed by this new revelation. "Are you trying to tell me that the spirit of Jack the Ripper is loose somewhere in London?"

He chuckled. "Now I understand why Holmes said that one thing leads to another. No, the Ripper spirit has been sent to hell where he belongs. How, you might ask? Because they lured it to Ireland, and Saoirse called down the banshees to drag him off to the underworld."

"Okay, this is a joke," she said, shaking her head. "This is some kind of perverse joke on Sage's part…"

"I'm afraid not. Ask yourself why she might do that. And how did she change all of the books in your electronic reader? How did she get your friend on the night desk to respond the way she did? It's too much to be able to pull off a scam like that, and why would she do that to you?"

"How do you know about the books, or about my friend at work?"

"Because, as I said, I didn't believe even for a

minute that you had bought Sage's story, so I monitored your electronic reader and your phone."

"You listened in on my phone call?"

"Yes, and then I slipped away from Holmes and Rachel's place and came back to try to reassure you and answer any questions you have."

Corinne held up a hand. "Let's just say, for a moment, that I believe any of this. You can explain how Sage, Rachel and Saoirse know, but what about Gabe and Anne?"

"Gabe has always been of your world, but he didn't know about the others… at least not at first. His first clue that supernatural things were possible was when they fought the Ripper. Gabe saw it. When Anne came along, they had no choice but to tell him."

"There's no ongoing female character named Anne in any of the Clive Thomas books."

"Although much has been written about dear Anne, she was never a character, but rather a woman who had been ill-used in her time and who, when she was murdered, refused to be shuffled off into the Light. When a chance came to escape the Void, she did."

"You're trying to tell me Anne is a ghost?" Corinne stared at him, wondering what was happening here. "Not buying it. I've spent time with her, bumped into her…"

He shook his head. "Not a ghost; not a reincarnation; something distinct and different. She has existed in two very different time periods."

What he is saying can't be true. And yet, if it was, it explained so much about her.

She looked at him, taking in a deep breath. "So far, you haven't prevaricated with me; please don't do so now."

Eddy nodded. "The woman you know as Anne Hastings, now Anne Watson, was once known by another name…"

"A woman who has nothing good to say about Henry VIII. Are you trying to tell me that Gabe's wife used to be Anne Boleyn?" She whispered the question, not sure what to think anymore.

"She was, although suffice it to say she's much happier with her second husband."

"Well, duh, as far as I know he doesn't have the power to cut her head off. Oh God, please don't tell her I said that. It's in incredibly bad taste."

"You underestimate your friend. She makes jokes about it all the time. For what it's worth, I think they will be relieved that you know."

Her eyes turned toward the window, toward Trafalgar Square. "Do they know about my aunt and her crazy tales about Big Ben?"

"Not so crazy. And if there wasn't at least a part of you that believed, you wouldn't have taken all those lessons."

"You mean she wasn't crazy?"

Eddy placed his hands gently on hers. "I'm afraid not. Search your feelings—haven't you felt like something was shifting?"

"Maybe…"

"There is no maybe. I'm sure you have, but at least now you have friends who will not think you are crazy and will be there to help. Saoirse is a powerful witch and a good ally to have."

Corinne thought about Saoirse, and then it hit her. "The little girl in the yellow dress? The girl from the time of Queen Victoria?"

"Yes. She and her friends were trapped by an evil man named Gull who thought what he did was in service of his queen. Our friends, led by Saoirse, were able to free her spirit and that of four other little girls who were killed with her."

"Holy shit."

He frowned at her. "I would prefer it if you wouldn't curse."

Corinne sat back. "Really? You would prefer? Why?"

"It is beneath you. You have a doctorate and will be working at one of the most prestigious museums in the world."

Not liking to feel rebuked, she said, "I don't know that you have any right to tell me that, nor am I inclined to listen."

Eddy's sexy grin was almost her undoing. He really was sex on a stick.

"If I have my way, neither of those statements will be true for very much longer."

Unsure of how to respond, she asked, "Now what?"

"Have I answered all your questions?"

"Yes."

He patted her hand again, reassuringly. "Then I will let you get some sleep. As you heard earlier, our queen has spoken, and Anne can get testy when we peasants don't follow her orders."

"I don't think Anne is like that at all," said Corinne, defending her friend.

"Nor do I. Rachel, Sage, Saoirse and Anne's friendships with you are real. I may take some flak from Roark, Gabe, and Holmes over having told you without speaking to them first, but Spense and the girls will be on my side."

"Okay. Then, I guess I'll see you a little later today."

"*Bien.*"

Eddy rose from the couch and headed toward the door.

"Eddy?" He turned to look at her. "Are you into the D/s lifestyle—you know, like you were in the books?"

His grin deepened, and his gaze grew dark and hot as he studied her. "*Oui*, and I have some of the same kinks as my character. I would very much like to show you around that world and even scene or play with you, depending on your level of interest."

Corinne could feel the heat creeping up her cheeks. On more than one occasion, she had imagined doing a lot of the things Eddy did in the books with Eddy himself. At first, she had skimmed over those parts of Sage's books, embarrassed by them perhaps or just not sure what to think of them. But more and more, they appealed to her, and she'd begun to wonder what it might be like to explore the pleasure that could be had at Baker Street. She knew about the place because it was something guests of the Savoy asked about all the time. And then she'd learned that the four couples whose relationships she most envied and found the most intriguing were all members.

She said nothing to Eddy about it, though. After he left, she slowly closed the door before sitting down to assess the situation. Well, if nothing else, she had information. Eddy had been right. Something inside her had felt as though things were changing in London, and not in a good way. If she believed Eddy, and she did, then she could no longer deny what her aunt had told her.

After her friends had finished getting her moved, she needed to talk at the very least to Saoirse and Eddy. If Big Ben was getting ready to strike thirteen and the lions were going to awaken at her command, she'd damn well better know what the hell she was doing.

Her mind drifted to the biggest surprise of the day. So, Eddy Chastain, her favorite book boyfriend, now existed in the real world. Hopefully, all that time and attention Anne had spent helping her select lingerie was not in vain. She shook her head, trying to wrap it around the fact three men her memory said she'd known for years had only come into physical existence a little more than a year ago.

It was insane to contemplate it, but in the marrow of her bones she felt it was true. Even if she accepted the incredible, she still had so many unanswered questions. She wondered if she'd ever know all the answers and then wondered if she even cared.

As for exploring D/s with Eddy? That sent a shiver of a whole different kind down her spine.

CHAPTER 13

*E*ddy slipped back into the townhouse. He'd been surprised that he knew how to drive. He hadn't figured it would be difficult, but still it had been nice to see that yet another skill of his had easily transferred into the real world with him. He knew he needed to tell his friends what he'd done, but he felt it needed doing if for no other reason than he didn't want to start his relationship with Corinne on a lie.

Already he had her at a disadvantage. He knew so much about her, and she knew so little about him. He'd spent more than a year keeping tabs on her. At first, just because she intrigued him. The more he'd learned, though, the more he'd wanted to know. Intellectual interest had turned to lust and then lust to arousal and more tender feelings. When Spense had asked him to keep an eye on her, he'd been more than happy to do so. It hadn't taken his friends long to figure out that Eddy's interest in Corinne had grown into more than just a passing fancy.

The death of her aunt and the legacy she left behind had fascinated him too, and now he was glad he'd indulged himself. Both he and Saoirse were convinced that there was something knocking at the gates of the portal below the Clock Tower. Having two swords from the Knights of the Round Table and warriors who knew how to wield them would be helpful in whatever fight was coming. As for the Landseer lions, whether they would help or hinder remained to be seen.

Ah, Corinne! Being near her was an exquisite form of torture. Being able to touch her, to smell her essence and if he was right, the first inkling of arousal, was heaven. Not being able to fold her in his arms to reassure and seduce her was a kind of torture. All he'd wanted to do from the moment he'd laid eyes on her was to strip her naked, take her to bed and sink his cock all the way up to his balls into her. God, he was almost as bad as Roark had been about Sage. He usually had at least one monitor devoted to Corinne at any hour of the day. He did try to respect her privacy… at least in the physical sense.

When she'd begun to research the D/s lifestyle and then Baker Street itself, Eddy had wanted to cheer. He liked telling himself the impetus to join his friends in the real world had been based on the shifting fields of energy both he and Saoirse could feel, but if he was being honest, that was only part of it. Eddy always knew he would never be truly happy in a strictly vanilla relationship. As Corinne read more and more of Sage's novels that delved in D/s—whether she called it that or laced it through a paranormal novel disguised as world-building—he'd begun to hope that they might find common ground there.

"You know, I'm feeling a bit like a parent waiting up for my errant teenage son," said Holmes, arms crossed, as Eddy entered the townhouse via the back entrance. "Just tell me you didn't wreck my SUV."

Eddy grinned. "Not at all. Not so much as a honked horn. It seems those skills came through with me as well."

"You went back and told her everything, didn't you?" Eddy nodded. "Even about Anne?"

"I didn't feel like I had a choice. I'm telling you, something is getting ready to come through that clock face. We're going to need her, and I think she needs to know the truth."

"I don't blame you. I felt the same way about Rachel. I remember thinking I should tell her before we got involved, but things just moved too fast, and we were together before I could come clean. But it's different for you."

"How so?"

Holmes shook a finger at him. "You're already in love with her."

"I never said that," protested Eddy.

"You didn't have to. You're a lousy liar and I'm a great detective."

"I want to be with her so badly, it hurts… literally. But I know I have to let her set the pace. I know so much more about her than she does me."

"Not really," said Holmes. "Sage wrote you very true to who you are, and you have always been her favorite character. Rachel said she wants to visit Baker Street, so that's an added bonus."

"I think we need to get through whatever's coming before I take her off to a kink club."

"Maybe. But I wouldn't hesitate to get involved with her."

"Certainly, I will take this time to get to know her and …"

Holmes shook his head. "No. If Corinne is who you want—and I have no doubt about that—I say seduce her; coerce her; do whatever it takes to bind her to you so tightly that when you say jump, she does it without hesitation. If whatever's coming is as bad as you and Saoirse think, we're going to need her to function as part of the team in order to beat it back. She needs to look at you as her champion—the one guy who can shield her from the darkness… even if you aren't sure it's true. She needs you to be sure."

"In other words, she needs a Dom."

"No. She needs *you* to be *her* Dom. Switching

topics, what do you think about the lions at Trafalgar Square coming to life?"

It was a big question, and one that Eddy didn't yet have all the answers for. "That's the one thing the legends and stories all agree on," he said. "But after that, they diverge into polar opposites. One group of tales says they'll destroy the city; the other that they'll protect it. Her aunt said protect. We'll need her to wake the lions but be ready for them to turn on us. I'm hoping we can wake them one at a time, to control them better."

Holmes ran a hand through his hair, thinking. "How the hell are we going to keep them hidden? I know Saoirse can raise a fog off the Thames…"

"At least both sites are relatively close to the water, and harder for people to see, especially if things happen at night. But I also know Saoirse is working on a couple of things to keep things hidden." He paused, considering his words. "Her power is kind of scary."

It was Holmes' turn to chuckle. "If she wasn't so firmly entrenched on our side, I might worry more. What do you know about Holcroft?"

"The fight master? Just that he's really good at his craft. Why?"

"In addition to the sword and bow, Corinne has a quarterstaff and a halberd. I've done some work with the latter. Roark and I thought we might go get some training."

"I can handle the bow if it'll let me."

"You mean if she'll let you…"

"No. Corinne can be foolish, but she isn't stupid. She knows she can only handle one weapon at the time, so asking her to give up the bow, quarterstaff and halberd for us to use shouldn't take a lot of persuading. But if that bow is what I think it is, it will only allow itself to be used by those it feels some kinship too. Otherwise, it'll turn its power on the person trying to use it."

"What do you mean *what it is*? It's a bow."

"It's more than that; if I'm correct, the bow is Storm Shadow. It has a history and backstory similar to Courechouse and Galatine."

Holmes shook his head. "I just wanted a chance to talk to you before we got started in the morning. If you want, we can fix up the gatehouse, but I'm kind of hoping you'll end up in Corinne's bed."

"That makes two of us," admitted Eddy. "A room here with you and Rachel is fine if I won't be imposing."

"Not at all; the townhouse is more than big enough. I'll see you in the morning."

∽

"What do you mean, you bloody well told her everything?" snarled Roark the next morning.

The group was gathered outside Rachel and

Holmes' place, standing in their drive, as Eddy explained what happened the night before.

"Sweetheart, calm down," Sage soothed. "This is Corinne we're talking about. It's not like he took out an ad in the newspaper."

"Are you all right with this?" Gabe asked Anne.

"Far more than you I suspect. Corinne would never betray any of us, and it sounds like she has as much to lose as we do," Anne replied.

"I think Saoirse and Eddy ought to go to Corinne's so the three of them can start putting their heads together and see if they can't figure out what's coming and how to stop it," offered Rachel. "Sweetheart, have you gotten any hits on that screenshot Eddy sent you?"

"That's the interesting thing. I did," said Holmes. "Small-town thief and arsonist for hire. Strictly third tier. We put out notice that he was a person of interest. One of the leads led us to him. He'd been attacked and had his throat ripped out."

"The local constabulary wants to write it off as an animal attack," said Holmes.

"Maybe it is," said Spense.

"In the city center? In a flat with a locked door? Hardly," snorted Holmes.

"And then again, maybe not. But I do like your idea of dropping off Eddy and Saoirse at Corinne's," said Spense.

"I agree," said Saoirse, looking at her husband

with an arched brow. "Not that any of you bothered to ask."

"They didn't ask me either," offered Eddy.

"That's because you're in love with her and they knew the answer, but I do think we should pool what we know and see where that takes us."

Again using two SUVs, they split the group in half. Gabe and Anne took Saoirse and Eddy to Corinne's flat, stopping at a bakery to pick up savory and sweet croissants to share with everyone. There was also coffee to go for those meeting at the flat above the Indian restaurant. Corinne was waiting and let them in as soon as they arrived.

Looking at the box of croissants, Corinne asked, "Aren't we all going?"

"We thought it might be better if you, Eddy and I put our heads together and tried to make some sense of what we do know, while the others pick up your remaining things," said Saoirse. "I'm hoping both of you have more concrete details to offer because honestly, all of my knowledge is kind of ethereal. I just feel as though there's something out there. Something that wants to get through to this dimension."

"Mine is based on nothing more than things my aunt said to me."

"She was clear about the thirteen chimes?" asked Saoirse.

Corinne nodded, inviting Eddy and Saoirse to take a seat so they could all talk. "Yes, at midnight instead of twelve, Big Ben will chime thirteen times. She told me I'm to take Galatine and go to Nelson's statue and tap the nose of the Landseer lion closest to the Clock Tower. His name is Wellington."

"Do the others have names?" asked Saoirse.

"Does it matter?" asked Eddy.

Saoirse nodded. "Yes. Many times in the supernatural world if you know something's name, it gives you a certain amount of power over it. So, knowing their names may be critical."

"I don't know which one is which, but the other three names are Victory, Napoleon and Nelson."

"Those all have to do with the war with Bonaparte and his eventual defeat," said Eddy. "My information is the fact that I can't find the information. I start trailing after something that sounds promising and either a big brick wall falls in front of me, or I find myself spiraling down a rabbit hole that leads to another dead end. It was one of the reasons I started thinking about coming out. More and more, I found myself being blocked and it didn't feel right... if you know what I mean."

"I know the Clock Tower is supposed to be built over some kind of supernatural portal, but I have no idea what triggers it or how we can stop it from ever opening," said Corinne. "Now that I don't think my aunt was completely off her rocker at the end, I wish I'd paid more attention."

"Is there anything you can think of that she specifically mentioned and that you ignored at the time? Some small thing that you dismissed as completely unimportant? When casting spells, it can be the details that make up all the difference."

"She did talk about the fact that the clock faces weren't one solid piece of glass—that they'd had to break them into shards and then piece them back together."

Eddy brought out his laptop and pulled up a close-up of Big Ben. "Did she say shards and break? Or did she say pieces? Because when I look at the face, the glass looks like it was cut into hundreds of specific pieces."

He watched as Corinne's beautiful face showed concentration and then enlightenment.

"You're right. She didn't say shards. I interpreted it that way. She did say pieces and talked about fitting them back together."

Saoirse nodded. "If Merlin was your ancestor…"

"And as far as I can tell, your family roots go back that far and he could very well have been," interrupted Eddy.

"Then it would make sense that he would reach out across time in a more precise way," added Saoirse.

"I thought he was sealed in some kind of crystal cave…"

Saoirse fluttered her hands. "Some believe Morgan Le Fay trapped him within a crystalline structure, but over time, crystals can lose some of their cohesion and crack, allowing him a way out at least for a brief period of time before the crystal heals itself."

"So, you think Merlin had a hand in the creation of Big Ben?"

Eddy smiled. "Big Ben is actually the bell itself. The clock tower and the clock were built to hold it. So, what if some demon or dark wizard—maybe even Morgan Le Fay—created the portal and Merlin got the clock tower built? If he knows his descendants are going to be in this fight, he has to have a way to warn them. And he has to limit how the demons can escape."

"If they are shapeless or can shift their shape to pass through the cracks, it might make them more vulnerable and give his descendants the time they need to fight it," added Saoirse, nodding excitedly.

"And knowing those who would follow him and wield Galatine, which is the shadow blade to Excalibur, would be a woman, he might think she needed help," added Corinne, "and he might enchant the bronze statues." She turned to Saoirse. "Could he do that?"

"I couldn't, but if Merlin was as powerful as they say, then yes he could."

"So, it will happen when it's dark, but London is a vibrant city. It never truly sleeps. Somebody's going to see four seven-ton lions roaming around London with a woman wielding an ancient, magickal sword," said Corinne.

"I can probably handle keeping it hidden, and I have no doubt you and your four lions could defeat a single demon, but I worry about what happens if there are more."

"She won't be alone, for one thing" insisted Eddy. "The demon realm would have no way of knowing about Gabe and Courechouse. Roark and Holmes are going to work with your instructor to sharpen their skills with the quarterstaff and halberd, respectively, if you'll entrust the weapons to them," he explained.

"Of course," Corinne said. "I have to tell you, I won't mind having a powerful witch, another swordsman and two other warriors on my side. I wonder…"

"Wonder what?" asked Eddy.

"There are four weapons, four of us and four lions—that seems significant and not coincidental," pondered Corinne, who suddenly turned to Eddy. "In the books, Eddy's… your favorite form of exercise was archery. He was an expert. Are you?"

"I am. The question is, will Storm Shadow accept me as her master?"

"You know about my bow?"

"I'm an archer and a geek—I know a great deal about a lot of famous and legendary bows. Are there any arrows with it? I ask because the same family of fletchers have been making the arrows for it since it was created."

"Yes. There's a bundle in the quiver and another bundle inside the case."

"Almost fifty arrows… That should be enough."

"What did you mean about Storm Shadow accepting you?" asked Saoirse.

"There are some nasty tales about that bow. She can't be strung unless she recognizes her master and if you try to force it, there's a carved dragon's tail on the bottom which will animate, wrapping itself around your forearm and trapping you. Then the head on the other end will come alive and breathe fire on you, burning you to a crisp."

Corinne's eyes widened.

"What is it?" asked Saoirse.

"There are black marks on the limbs of the bow. Do you suppose they're char marks?"

"Most likely," said Eddy. "The thing is, Storm Shadow is said to be able to hit a target at more than twice the normal distance. A normal bow can fire less than half a mile, but Storm Shadow is said to be able to fire more than twice that."

"If you took up a position on Nelson's pillar, you could cover the rest of us as we travel from Trafalgar Square to Big Ben."

"Might I point out here that you are also an excellent archer. You could cover Roark, Spense, Holmes and me from a safe distance," argued Eddy.

"But you are not the Sentinel of the Portal," Corinne said "I am. And I alone can awaken the lions and, I would think, control them."

"I don't like it. It's too dangerous," grumbled Eddy.

"What you don't like," Corinne said, leaning over and putting her hand on his knee, "is that I'm right and you know it."

He looked down at her hand. He could feel the heat from her body pass to his, and his cock came to life. His entire system lit up from the rush of arousal that surged through him. All she had to do was touch him, and he didn't give a damn about demons. All he wanted was to be with her to get inside her. He wanted to fuck her like he'd wanted nothing else in his life. There was an angel on his shoulder telling him to slow down and to think about the job they had to do. The devil on his other shoulder had a direct line to his cock and was saying that if they were going to die in order to save humanity, they might as well fuck first.

Eddy was inclined to listen to the devil… It was the one he knew better.

CHAPTER 14

It didn't take long for the others to join them, bringing up the last of her personal items. They all looked at Corinne expectantly while trying not to be obvious.

She decided to address the manner straight on. "Last night, Eddy shared with me some of the stuff that's been going on with all of you. I have to admit at first I was hurt that you hadn't known absolutely that you could trust me…" As protestations to the contrary started, Corinne raised her hand. "And then I realized, you could say the same of me. That got me to thinking why that had been the case, and I realized that at least for me, I didn't want you to think my aunt or I was a certified crazy person. Magickal swords, banshees hauling the Ripper to Hell, freeing the spirits of those little girls—that was wonderful, by the way—finding your way out of the pages of a book, bronze lions coming to life—it wasn't that we questioned each other's trust, but rather the sanity of the one telling the tale… or at least that the one being told might."

"I'm so glad you understand," said Sage. "I think for all of us, it's been kind of a learning experience. Who do you tell? When do you tell them? Things like that. I have to hand it to Eddy; he handled it better than the rest of us."

Corinne laughed. "For me, strange as this may sound, the weirdest part was finding Eddy replaced by Elias in the books, less than twenty-four hours after I'd last read one. And nobody else knows there's been a change?"

Sage shook her head. "No. The change seems to happen instantaneously in the e-books and paper and hardbacks, in the audiobooks and in everyone's mind. If you think it's weird for you, think about it from my standpoint. I remember what I wrote, but when I go back to read it, it's different."

"I've never thought to ask," said Rachel. "Does it bother you?"

"I don't know that bother is the right word, but it is disconcerting. And as fantastical as this has all been, I think the thing I find the most fascinating is Anne. I've always wanted to know…" The rest of the group groaned.

"What's that for?" laughed Corinne.

"Whenever Sage starts a sentence like that, it means she's gone into writer research mode," replied Anne. "So, what about my execution do you want to know?"

"Did it hurt? I mean, did you feel it and know you were dying?"

"Obviously, I can't speak for anyone else, but I think the one kindness Henry did show me was the French swordsman. I didn't feel anything. He was so quick and so sure with his stroke that he severed my head completely with a swift blow. I don't think my mind even had time to recognize pain, and there sure wasn't a moment when my head was severed that I realized I had been executed."

Corinne watched as the former Queen of England, who was sitting in her husband's lap, stroked down his back, not to further her connection to him or to comfort herself but to ease his tension and pain. The fact that Gabriel Watson was distressed by what she'd said was obvious.

"It's fine, sweetheart," Anne soothed. "It was a very long time ago and had it not happened the way it did, I wouldn't be here now sitting in your lap. And I wouldn't change that for anything."

Gabe drew her close, nuzzling her neck. "He was a bastard and a fool."

Anne grinned. "Yes, he was and not anywhere close to as good in the sack as you."

Everyone laughed, and Corinne wondered if

Anne had been gifted with her easy charm and innate kindness during Tudor times. After working to get Corinne completely unpacked and settled in her new flat, the group all agreed to head home, get cleaned up and adjourn to Holmes and Rachel's townhouse for dinner, after which they'd get everyone up-to-speed on Corinne's situation.

As she closed the door after the last of her friends were gone, Corinne leaned back against it looking at her flat and smiled. Her Aunt Peggy would have liked her new place. She could easily hear Big Ben and was close to Trafalgar Square. More than that, at the end of her moving day, her flat looked like home. It was as if she'd been settled in for months if not years. It was good to have friends.

~

Eddy grinned as he trudged up the stairs in Holmes' townhouse. His friends had warned him that even though he was healthy, fit and Sage had described him as strong and muscular, in the world beyond the Veil, he would have to contend with the reality of never having had corporeal form. His muscles ached and he was tired, something else he'd never experienced before. Yet he'd never felt better in his life.

He was once again in the same realm as his friends. He'd been transparent and honest with

Corinne, and she didn't hate him. More than that, they'd gotten a lot accomplished and he felt that she was safe.

The knock on the door came slightly before it cracked open, and Holmes stuck his head in. "Are you feeling all right?"

"Tired and sore, but happy to be here."

"A good hot shower should help with that. Were the three of you able to figure anything out?"

"Holmes," Eddy could hear Rachel behind him, "let the poor man take a shower. You can wait to hear everything with the rest of us. Come take a shower with me."

"That's got to be a pretty good incentive," teased Eddy.

Holmes grinned. "You have no idea. You're on your own until the rest of them get here."

Eddy laughed as Holmes headed down the hall to join his wife. Holmes was a changed man. He'd always been in charge; always been a Dom and liked to control every aspect of his life in a serious and forthright manner. Rachel had softened the edges. He was still tough and strong, but he smiled more often, and her very presence seemed to give solace to the venerable DSI. While he had no doubt that Holmes was the dominant partner in his marriage, it seemed that Rachel had a way of wrapping him around her finger and making him happy.

Eddy's cock was throbbing as he undressed. It had been fully engorged most of the day. Just being around Corinne affected him in a strongly visceral way. While adrenaline and arousal had raced through his body, he'd been hard most of the day. When she'd chosen to sit next to him, it had taken every ounce of self-control not to, at the very least, pull her into his lap to breathe in her scent. An aroma which he'd been able to discern had an increasing note of arousal in it. He liked thinking that she wanted him too.

He stripped and entered the bath, turning on the water to let it heat up. He grinned, imagining that Holmes was going to enjoy his shower far more than he was. Once he'd removed the jeans Rachel had purchased for him yesterday, his unruly cock sprang free. He'd wondered if he'd have the same physical abilities, especially in matters of sex, as Sage had described in her books. It would appear he had.

Knowing he would be coming through the Veil with literally only the clothes on his back, Rachel had done a bit of shopping for him, so he'd have something to wear. Holmes really had found himself the most wonderful woman, and Eddy had hoped he would be so lucky. He'd found her; he just needed to convince her that they were right for each other.

Stepping into the hot, steamy shower, Eddy realized that as hot and wet as it was, he was planning on getting Corinne even hotter and wetter. He shook his head, reminding himself there were larger, more important things to think about than fucking Corinne, but at the moment his hard cock couldn't think of a single one.

The idea of not only getting inside Corinne and hearing her call out his name as she came, but of building a life with her, made everything else pale in comparison. Somehow the idea of fighting off a demon and re-sealing a portal into another dimension just seemed like an insignificant roadblock if it meant a future with Corinne was on the other side.

Sage had written him as a loner, but she had been wrong. It wasn't that Eddy liked being isolated; it was just that a lot of what he did was better off done without anyone hanging around. He longed to have what his friends had—a sexy partnership with a woman who shared his life in all ways.

A part of Eddy wanted to grab Corinne by the hand and run away with her—far from whatever was coming through that gateway. But he knew neither of them could ever abandon their friends, and they each had a part to play in the upcoming battle. His cock argued that if they were going to die, they at least ought to do it after having fucked each other silly. Eddy couldn't disagree with his cock.

Stepping under the shower, Eddy allowed himself the luxury of indulging all of his senses—the feel of the heat, the sensation of the hot water rolling down his body, the smell of the shampoo as he opened it and used it in his hair. Then he opened the bottle of shower gel and used the large sea sponge to cleanse his body. It felt amazing. His cock throbbed as if to remind him that it had never had real pussy and it wanted it now—and not just any pussy, but Corinne's.

He turned the water to cold to rinse off, hoping the sudden change in temperature would shock his body into behaving. It was a complete and utter failure. Instead of withering up and seeking the warmth of his body cavity, the damn thing got stiffer and began to drip a bit of pre-cum. He wondered if he ought to somehow mark this day as the first time he got off in the real world.

Eddy wrapped his hand around his stiff shaft and began to stroke. He was finding that all the sensations he'd enjoyed on the other side of the Veil felt intensified on this side. He took long, even strokes from the bulbous head back to where that body part joined his body. While it felt good, he was quite certain it would be far more pleasurable when it was Corinne's pussy squeezing along his whole length. He idly wondered if Roark knew about Sage's obsession with large cocks.

He closed his eyes and imagined having Corinne beneath him. He would get her completely aroused, maybe even letting her come, before settling himself between her legs and driving his shaft deep inside her. It was easy to fantasize that it was her sheath contracting all around him, fighting to keep him inside when he took control, dragging his cock almost all the way out before plunging back inside. He would make her come several times before finally burying himself all the way to his hilt and pumping her full until he had no more to give her. He stroked himself faster and harder until his whole body stiffened, and he came, covering his fist with his warm semen and allowing the water to wash it away.

Eddy turned the water back from cold to warm and finished up before turning it off completely, getting out and using the soft, fluffy towels to dry off. He luxuriated in the feel of the cloth as it ran across his naked flesh, removing all the excess water. Checking his face in the mirror, he decided to forego shaving as he rather liked the sexy, disheveled image staring back at him.

Humming a jaunty little tune from his nonexistent childhood, Eddy got dressed. He had to admit Holmes' wife had excellent taste in men's clothing. He grinned thinking about Holmes telling him that Rachel herself had favored dowdy clothing before they met. He had been laughing when he relayed the story of how Anne had completely obliterated her wardrobe, told him she was going to spend lots of his money, and taken Rachel shopping. Fortunately, Corinne had already been subjected to the Anne Watson makeover. And if she could transfer her skills with her friends to clients on their wedding day, her bespoke wedding gown business was going to be a smashing success.

Having finished dressing, Eddy ran down the

stairs to answer the door, hollering over his shoulder that Holmes didn't need to hurry. If the look on his friend's face had been any indication, DSI Holmes would not have wanted to be rushed. Eddy wasn't the least bit surprised when it was Corinne at the door.

CHAPTER 15

She looked glorious—not at all like a woman who had spent the day unpacking and getting settled into her new flat. She had on patterned black leggings and a baggy sweater in a deep cinnamon color that complimented them. He liked the way that while the sweater was loose-fitting, it seemed to cling lightly to her curves, and the deep V-neck offered a tantalizing view to someone tall enough to enjoy it. If he looked down, he could easily see the valley between her tits, as well as the slight swell of the side of the breasts that formed it.

"Am I early? No one else seems to be here," she said by way of greeting.

"Holmes and Rachel are upstairs; I'm sure the others will be along any time. I'm not overly familiar with the house yet, but I'll bet we can find the kitchen and the bar. What do you say we help ourselves?"

Corinne held up a small brown bag with twisted raffia handles. "I come bearing gifts. There's the most wonderful cheese shop by my house, and I couldn't resist. All kinds of creamy, gooey goodness. They had crackers as well."

Eddy wanted to give her creamy, gooey goodness but it had nothing to do with cheese. He forced himself to put those thoughts on hold. Their time would come, he was sure of it. They made their way back to the kitchen, put together a passable cheese tray, grabbed a couple of long-neck microbrews and went into the sitting room.

"I love these old Georgian places, but this isn't what I expected, and yet it is," she said.

"What do you mean?"

"When I look through magazines, they're always so formal and elegant. This has the elegance of the architecture, but the furniture and furnishings are more casual, and you can imagine feeling comfortable here and having a place to put your feet up."

Eddy looked around; she was right. "I'd never thought about that, but I can see what you're saying. The pictures of similar townhouses are stiff and lovely to look at, but it's hard to imagine actually living there. Everything about this place that I've seen so far speaks to comfort and livability. I think it's one of the things I liked about your place—it's easy to imagine wanting to spend a lot of time there."

"Would you like to spend time there… with me, I

mean?" she said a frown, marring the perfection of her face.

Eddy placed the cheese tray on the low table in front of the couch, and taking the bottles from her hand, he set them down beside the tray. Then he gazed into her eyes, with a smile. "Very much so."

Her countenance brightened. "Oh good. I'd like that too."

She sat down on the couch, drawing her legs and feet up underneath her and seemed happy when he settled in next to her. He twisted off the top of her microbrew and handed her the bottle before doing the same to his. They tipped their bottles to one another in a mock salute, and each took a long sip.

"That's good," she sighed.

"Yes. Far better than when I used to do it in the book."

"What do you mean?"

"When I first became sentient, I experienced things that happened in the book, but what I'm finding on this side of the Veil is that those feelings and sensations are greatly intensified."

"It makes me sad to think you only got to experience a kind of half-life in the book."

"Only for the past year or so. Before then I wasn't aware of anything, so even the mildest of sensations was an improvement. I had some time to adjust to that before coming through the Veil and experiencing everything at full strength. I wonder if it wasn't almost painful for the others."

"Why did you choose to remain behind?" she asked.

"At first, because I didn't have a clue how to change it. Remember, Roark pierced the Veil to save Sage. We're still not sure how Spense and Holmes found themselves on this side. Luckily for Spense, he didn't emerge as described in the books."

"How was he described?"

"Not as handsome as he is now."

"Oh, dear. I'm sure Saoirse is glad he looks the way he does, although in all honesty I'm not sure it would really matter, other than she very much enjoys the physical side of their relationship."

"Yes, I would say that all three of my friends' wives enjoy the pleasure provided to them by their husbands. I know for a fact their husbands enjoy that part of their marriages immensely." He shook his head.

"What?" she asked.

"As you know, the men in Sage's books are very sexual. In fact, Roark was a bit of a manwhore. Each book featured a new woman for him to save, spank and fuck."

"I know. It's part of the allure of those books… so much sexy, spanking fun."

"But even though the books have remained the same, Roark himself is a far different man than the character he was or that Clive is. He is deeply in love with Sage, and I think there's a part of him that wishes he had behaved differently before he came to life."

"He shouldn't. For one thing, it was before he knew Sage. For another, he was a fictional character in the books. And last, she should have nothing to complain about. After all, she created him."

"That's very true." Switching the subject, he turned to the topic that intrigued him most—the beautiful woman seated beside him. "I know you were born in Cornwall. Did your legacy bring you to London?"

"No," Corinne answered. "I came up here to attend college, fell in love with the city and decided to get my doctorate. My family had disowned my aunt when I was a child, and my mother was furious when she found out my aunt had reached out to me and that I was visiting with her."

He took another sip of beer, watching her. "That must have made it difficult for you."

"Not really. I mean, I was at that stage in my life where you kind of want to rebel and this was a really safe, fun way to do it. My aunt was a lot of fun and when she wanted me to learn to use the weapons, it just seemed like a quirky request. But it was fun and a great form of exercise. It wasn't until she was dying that she told me the real reason why. The funny thing is, given the way my mother talked about her, I was surprised that my aunt never said a word against her. At the end, she did say that my mother held my aunt responsible for their mother's death. I'm not exactly sure why, and my mother won't discuss it at all. My aunt's funeral was rather sad."

"Aren't all funerals inherently sad?"

Corinne snagged a piece of cheese and a cracker, munching while she thought. "Actually, I've been to several that were truly a celebration of someone's life, but there was only one other person at my aunt's. It bothered me a lot when I realized that if what she said was true, mine would be the same way."

"I disagree. You have a lot of friends who would miss you and would want to say goodbye."

"I feel better about that now. I understand now the choices she made, and unlike me, she didn't have anyone to share what she knew with, much less a group of people who were willing to stand with her."

"I'm glad you realize you are no longer alone and that your aunt carried a heavy burden."

Corinne sighed softly. "She really did. And I'm trying hard not to resent my family's letting her do that by herself."

"I don't think you can blame them," he said gently, taking her hand in his. "They either didn't understand or didn't believe, and she may not have felt as though she wanted to burden them as well."

"Could be. I just wish I'd been more supportive, taken more time to listen and learn. I know how much easier it has been for me to think about it now that it's out in the open with all of you. And by the way, my secret now sounds almost normal compared to the rest of you."

Eddy grinned. "*Oui*. We are a most curious group. It almost sounds like the start of a bad joke—a witch, a dead queen and four guys from out of a book walked into a bar…"

"Don't finish that," said Watson from behind them as he and Anne walked in from the back. "I can tell you for a fact that her majesty here felt anything but dead a little bit ago."

Anne rapped Watson's head from behind as she walked past him. "Honestly, Gabe, there are times I can't take you anywhere."

Watson grabbed his wife, wrapping her in his arms and pulling her close. "I only speak the truth, my beautiful queen."

Anne wound her arms around his neck and pressed herself against him. "You were pretty spectacular yourself," she purred.

As far as Eddy was concerned, Henry VIII had been a complete and utter fool. Within short order, they were joined by not only Rachel and Holmes, but Saoirse, Spense, Roark and Sage as well

"How are you feeling?" Anne asked Eddy. "I know when I first came through the Veil, it was a kind of sensory overload combined with exhaustion."

"I seem to be able to keep the exhaustion at bay,

and so far the sensory experience has all been of the good kind. Besides, I think had I waited, I would have been trapped."

"That was weird," said Gabe. "Could you see what was holding onto you?"

"Not really. I had the feeling that it was vaguely human, but not completely. There were fingers, but they felt more skeletal than fleshy. And there were only three fingers and a thumb-like appendage. I couldn't see it at all, but when I smashed it with my foot, the face felt smooshed in… the features not as distinct as a human skull."

"That doesn't sound good. Do you know where it came from or why it wanted to stop you?" asked Rachel.

"We think that whatever is planning to come through the clock face is pulling power from other dimensions. I think it sent that thing to stop me. My area had been collapsing—getting smaller and smaller. I knew I either needed to go or I would be trapped."

"Do you think it wanted the information on the laptop?" asked Corinne.

"Interesting question," Eddy mused. "I don't know that it wanted it for its own edification, but I do think it didn't want me to get through the Veil with it."

"You're a triple threat to it," said Saoirse. "You're the one most likely to be able to dig up information that we can use, and you are a master archer."

"That's only two things; you said *triple threat*," commented Corinne.

"Aye. I think they also know he's your protector."

"My what?"

"Your protector. I did some digging this afternoon and made a few phone calls. The Sentinel of the Portal has been in existence long before Big Ben or the lions. And we were wrong about why the Clock Tower was built. It wasn't built by the powers of Light. Morgan Le Fay was behind it. She means to open the door between the two realms to set her most powerful minions free. She means to remake the world in her image. She's been resting and gathering power."

"We're talking about King Arthur's half-sister, right?" asked Gabe.

"Half-sister, lover, high-priestess, sorceress—you name it, she's had it attached to her. One of the few consistent things about her is that in the end, she was instrumental in Arthur's death and in trapping Merlin in the crystal cave. He's never been able to escape completely, but over the millennia, he's been able to use astral projection to escape through cracks in the crystal for brief interludes to thwart some of her schemes."

As the others murmured in surprise, Corinne leaned in closer, eager to learn more of her heritage and calling. She urged Saoirse to explain further, and the Irish witch obliged.

"Did you know that originally the clock faces of Big Ben weren't supposed to have any protective glass?" Saoirse asked. "Something that big might have been able to focus enough light to keep the demons at bay. Every time they tried to lift a clock face up, it shattered. So Merlin designed an intricate, decorative pattern of cut pieces to enclose the different faces. They've been able to focus enough light to keep the portal closed, but this time Morgan Le Fay waited and gathered enough power."

"Why would she want the clock tower built to begin with?" asked Corinne.

"Most likely to concentrate the lack of light. She's tried to open the portal a couple of times and has wreaked havoc on London. The Great Fire of 1666—please note the 666 or number of the beast which comes up in a great many religions; the Black Plague beginning in 1665 and ending in 1666. There have even been those who thought the Aberfan Mine Disaster in 1966—again 66 and 9 flipped around is 6 —might be part of the pattern. And there are at least another fifteen to twenty instances of battles, mass executions or other natural disasters that could well have been Morgan trying to break free."

"Who records these things?" asked Eddy. "And why couldn't I find records of them?"

"Morgan is thorough and good at covering up or

redirecting her failures, so they don't come home to roost, so to speak. I decided to go directly to the source."

"You talked to Morgan Le Fay?" asked Sage, eyebrows raised in alarm.

Eddy shook his head, grinning at her. "She spoke to the Order of the Seven Maidens."

CHAPTER 16

Corinne looked between the two of them. "Dare I ask who the Order of the Seven Maidens might be?"

Saoirse gave her a smile. "The complete story is a long and complex one, but the short version is this: Originally, they were a group of nuns who were raped, left for dead and had their convent burnt out. Instead of conveniently dying so the church and all those who should have protected and cared for them could just wring their hands, they lived. And they followed the old adage that living well is the best revenge. They made a smashing success of their bees, brewing and farming. They were an integral part of the community. Some say they rivaled the Templars for wealth, and at one point the two entities were bitter enemies. They've been in league with Merlin, who is said to have saved them since the beginning.

They're also the ones who have been funding the Sentinel of the Portal all along."

Saoirse turned to Eddy and smiled. "If you're wondering, it was the Order that shut down your lines of inquiry into their doings. It was only when I told them you'd come from beyond the Veil to protect their Sentinel that they were willing to share information with me. They, too, are feeling that Morgan's next attempt to open the portal is imminent."

"My aunt never had a protector," said Corinne.

"Your aunt was never called to act. It seems the protector only shows up when the threat is looming."

"And?" said Anne suspiciously. "I know you, Saoirse. There's something you're not telling us."

"Yes, but I should probably talk to Corinne alone and let her decide…"

"Not necessary," said Corinne, waving the idea away and taking another sip of her drink. "I feel like you've all thrown in with me, and I don't want there to be any secrets. I'm new to being a part of this supernatural stuff, so I want everybody to know everything. You never know who's going to see something in a different way that leads us to making the right decision."

Saoirse nodded. "All right. The abbess was quite frank with me. She said the Sentinel and her Protector have always had a sexual relationship—sometimes without the initial consent of the Sentinel. Keep in mind that female consent, within the context of time immemorial, is a relatively new thing."

Eddy suddenly understood the true meaning and depth of the old saying: *the silence was deafening*. All those present sat not only silent, but completely still.

"Is that just because men were able to get away with that bullshit?" asked Corinne in an even tone of voice.

"Partly," said Anne. "That was the natural order of things. During much of our history, women had no power at all and very few could have defended themselves. Sometimes I wonder why I let my family manipulate me the way I did. The answer is because I had no other choices."

Gabe wrapped his arm around his wife, who snuggled into his warm comfort and assurance as she continued. "It's easy to sit in this beautiful townhouse, in this relatively tolerant era, and say I could have struck out on my own, but I couldn't have. It wasn't that I didn't want to be poor; I didn't want to die. I had been raised to serve my family's interests and to be the wife of a powerful noble. I had no training whatsoever to survive outside the safe walls of castles, manor houses and palaces."

"Then we shall have to find a new way," said Eddy.

"I hate to sound like the chauvinistic, patriarchal sonofabitch my wife often accuses me of being," said Roark.

"Only when you're acting like one," quipped Sage.

"But Anne is right; it was the natural order. And before every female in the room throws something at me, for the most part, it probably still should be. The problem is, a lot of men have offered up their dominance because it's a lot of fucking responsibility and work. I personally think it's worth it, but a lot of men got lazy and a lot of women, rightfully so, got angry. I have to say if I was a woman, I wouldn't just submit to any asshole who called himself a Dom. He'd damn well have to earn it and be worth it."

"You may well be a chauvinistic, patriarchal sonofabitch, but at least you're an enlightened one," said Sage, leaning over to kiss him. "And you're mine."

"In the interest of full disclosure, I spoke to Eddy last night…" started Holmes.

Rachel stood up, "And this, ladies, is when we leave the gentlemen to their brandy and cigars and go into the other sitting room and have a little girl-talk."

Holmes frowned at her. "Rachel, we talked about this."

"Yes, and I don't disagree with you. I just think you are about to botch this and make all of our guests feel awkward and uncomfortable."

With that, Rachel swept out of the room, followed by the other women, although Corinne looked back once at Eddy, as if curious to see his reaction before she, too, exited.

"What do you think that was all about?" asked Eddy when they were gone and out of earshot. The other men exchanged glances, and then Holmes shrugged.

"I think that was all about figuring out if Corinne is willing to submit to you," said Holmes. "If she's in..." He shrugged again, leaving the question open.

"Sage said Eddy was always her favorite character, and her body language seemed to indicate she was attracted to him," Roark pointed out.

"What happens if she says no?" asked Spense.

"Knowing our wives, we'll have to figure out how to fight this thing without the two of you being a couple," Holmes answered.

Eddy made a sharp, chopping gesture with his hand. "I'm telling you up front, there will be no non-consensual relationship."

Gabe chuckled. "There's consent and then there's consent." He held up his hand to stave off an argument. "I know, no means no. But I can tell you with Anne, no sometimes means, persuade me..."

"Or I want it, but I don't want to admit it," agreed Roark.

"But you're talking about women you've been with for a while now..." argued Eddy.

"But it's been true from the beginning," said Roark.

Holmes frowned. "Speak for yourself. I was very clear with Rachel from the beginning that she had to consent, and she had to understand what she was agreeing to. That works for us. But like everything else, each relationship has its own rules and evolves the way the couple wants and agrees to."

Spense agreed. "At least she knows going in what she's getting into and will have friends to help her along the way and answer questions she might have."

"But she needs to be looking to Eddy for those answers," said Gabe.

After that, the conversation drifted off, and each man sat looking at his drink, deep in silent contemplation.

~

Once the ladies were inside the other room, the library, Rachel closed and locked the door.

"So, what exactly did you and Holmes talk about?" asked Corinne, arms folded across her chest.

Rachel encouraged everyone to sit down, and then she explained. "He had a chance to talk to Eddy who, by the way, is crazy about you. I think it's really interesting that all of these men have a bad habit of hanging back, then declaring themselves and expecting you to go weak at the knees."

"Well, don't we?" asked Anne, arching her brow.

"It's so annoying," laughed Saoirse.

"I feel like I should apologize for writing them that way," admitted Sage.

"No need. It isn't your fault. Gabe wasn't one of your characters, and he's just like the rest of them," said Anne. "Which leads us to the first and most pertinent question… How do you feel about Eddy, Corinne?"

"Steamroller Anne strikes again," said Rachel, rolling her eyes. The other woman shrugged a shoulder.

"I don't think we have time to pussyfoot around this," she argued. "If she has feelings for Eddy…"

The idea of it all felt a bit overwhelming. Corinne took a deep sip of her drink, thinking. "I just met the man… And then I found out he truly used to be one of Sage's characters…"

"In a series of books you love," the author pointed out. "And you once told me that Eddy was actually your favorite character and your ultimate book boyfriend."

"Book boyfriend?" queried Anne, who occasionally was still stumped by new, modern terms.

"A character in a book that you most wish could be real and kind of fulfills all your fantasies about what the perfect boyfriend would be," explained Sage.

Anne snorted. "No wonder Gabe wasn't in the books."

Everyone laughed at that, and then Sage said, "Don't be too sure. Gabriel Watson is the stuff a lot of women fantasize about."

"Which brings us back to my original question: Corinne, do you have feelings for Eddy?"

The silence in the room was only broken by the rhythmic swinging of the pendulum of the mantle clock as the minutes ticked by.

"If he was interested…"

"Trust me," said Rachel gently, "there is no if."

"I agree," said Sage. "I've watched him evolve since the others got out. I think originally, he would have been inclined to stay on the other side of the Veil. His desire to come through the Veil has very little to do with the bogeyman that's getting set to come through the portal; it has even less to do with this thing collapsing his space. I am convinced, as is Roark, that he would have come through the Veil to be with you, even if he wasn't some kind of protector or you hadn't been in danger."

The others all nodded.

"I have to say, Holmes said pretty much the same thing to me last night after he talked with Eddy."

Corinne frowned. "Eddy might have thought to say something to me about it," she grumbled.

"I think that had to do with not wanting you to feel pressured. He's had a lot more time to get to know you than you've had to get to know him," said Saoirse.

"I agree," said Sage. "I think Eddy would have preferred to take it slow, to let you get to know him, to date you and all the normal stuff, but now he doesn't have that time."

Corinne turned to Anne. "You're being awfully quiet."

"I have a different take on it and regardless of what anyone thinks, I hope you know you have the full support of everyone in this room… and the men as well, including Eddy. But I have to say if he's supposed to be your protector and that gives us the best shot at stopping this thing, I'd be inclined to do whatever is needed."

"Anne, how can you say that? You who suffered because of your family and Henry. I thought you'd be…"

"What? An emotional mess? Did my family and Henry use me up and discard me? Yes, but in the end, I protected my daughter and my family by what I did. And let's be honest, I got to be Queen of England for a very short time. If she finds the prospect of fucking Eddy to be distasteful, then she shouldn't do it. Which once again begs the answer to my original question, do you have feelings for Eddy?"

"It's not that simple," equivocated Corinne.

"It is," said Anne, sitting down next to her and taking Corinne's hands in hers. "We can't proceed at all without the answer to that question."

"You can't just dump all this shit on me and say decide," argued Corinne, trying to draw away.

"Time has caught you up as it does most of us. It

may not be fair and may make you feel as though we're only heaping more stress on you, but it is the question you need to figure out—and quickly. If you don't, we'll ignore the precedents from the past, but if you do, then we need to move forward as rapidly as we can in a way that works for you."

Corinne searched Anne's face and realized the former queen was right, that more than anyone in the room, she was the one who understood the call of both duty and the heart. And if her duty had involved her heart all those years ago with King Henry, then that meant…

"You loved him once, didn't you?" asked Corinne.

Anne nodded. "Fool that I was, I did. And perhaps even more foolishly, I believe there was a time he loved me."

"Would you make the same choice?"

"If I'd never met Gabriel and was in the same situation? Yes."

Corinne shook her head. It was all happening so fast, and in such an unexpected way. "Forgive me," she asked Saoirse, "but what does sex have to do with being the Sentinel?"

"I don't think it's just sex, but rather dominant sex. Sex has a powerful magick all its own. I think probably the sex is used to bind the Sentinel to her Protector and vice versa. And the presence of dominance to ensure that she is in the habit of listening to him and doing what she's told," explained Saoirse.

"That makes sense," said Rachel. "You need to work together as a team to survive, Corinne. And in fact, Holmes said that to Eddy—that he needed to get close to you and use sex as a means to bind you to him so hopefully you'll listen, and you'll live through this."

Corinne nodded and then turned to Saoirse. "After this is over, I want to have a little chat with the Abbess of the Order of the Seven Maidens."

CHAPTER 17

They rejoined the men, who were waiting solemnly, and frankly a lot more quietly than Corinne would have expected. The more she thought about it, the more the idea of being with Eddy appealed to her—even if it was just for the duration of the fight. After all, he was supposed to be her *protector*, and she was interested in exploring the lifestyle of her friends.

"Hmm, I'm not sure how to interpret this little formation," said Holmes, watching them.

"I'd like to talk to Eddy alone," said Corinne.

"That's our cue, then," Holmes said. "I called in our dinner order. They should be here any time. I'll have them deliver to the kitchen. Come join us when you're done."

When they were alone, Eddy came to stand with her. Gently, he took her hand and led her back to the settee. "You need to understand that this is your call. We'll present it to the group as a joint decision. I will back whatever decision you make."

"Thank you. It's weird; I do feel like I know you and if I'm being honest, I would have to say that the idea of having sex with you is more than interesting… It's downright intoxicating."

Eddy chuckled. "Keeping an eye on you, to make sure you were safe, started as a favor to Spense and Roark. It was an easy favor to keep. Soon, I found myself watching you because I wanted to make sure you were safe. I tried to keep it at least semi-professional, but you are extremely beautiful and the idea of being with you is incredibly arousing."

"Okay, so we don't find each other repulsive."

"That may well be the grossest understatement I've ever heard." He laughed, a sound that sent a shiver of pleasure up her spine.

"The girls seemed to think I had a lot to learn in terms of the D/s lifestyle. I've been doing a lot of research since they took me shopping, but while I understand the theories and goals, I have zero real-life experience."

He cocked an eyebrow, a grin playing across his face. "I just stepped out of a book, you know…"

"But in the books, you were a long-time player."

"I don't want to play with you, Corinne." He pushed a lock of her soft blonde hair behind her ear.

His touch, though slight, warmed her to her core. "Yes, I know what I'm doing, and I can teach you…"

"The girls thought some classes at Baker Street might help," she confessed, feeling her cheeks heat.

Eddy nodded. "If you would feel more comfortable having some guided experiences in a place you know you would be safe, we can do that."

"You need to know if I didn't feel safe with you, there's no fucking way I'd do this—regardless of whatever big bad is coming."

Eddy frowned. "Watch your language…"

It was Corinne's turn to laugh. "They all said you'd get on me about my language."

"It's beneath you…"

"And gives you the perfect excuse to get your hands on my ass and spank me."

Eddy grinned and nodded as if to say *touché*. "That too."

He rose to his feet but prevented her from standing until he extended his hand to her. "Patience. I lead. You follow. You wait for me—to help you, to pull out your chair, to open the door…"

Corinne stared at him, surprised. "You do know I'm perfectly capable of doing all those things without you, and I swing a mean broadsword too."

"*Oui*. I am aware of both. I am also aware that from this point until you say we're done, I am the Dom, and you are my sub. Agreed?"

"Okay."

"*Non.* Not okay. Yes Sir, or yes Master."

"It's not like we're playing a role…"

"Not for the world to see, but we need to immerse ourselves in these roles, so that when push comes to shove, I know you'll do as I say. If you're not used to obeying me, it could be catastrophic not only for you but for our friends. Understand?"

"Yes, Sir."

Eddy grinned, "Good girl."

She was beginning to understand some of the things she'd read. All he'd said were two little words, and she'd felt a lovely warm shiver roll all through her body. She hadn't lied to him when she said she trusted him. The problem she worried about was, could she trust herself? At the end, would she have gone so far down this rabbit hole that if he wanted to leave, it would destroy her? At the end of the day though, did she have a choice?

They joined their friends in the large kitchen with the enormous harvest table. It was roughhewn and rustic with a smooth matte finish. There was heavy hand-forged iron work acting as legs to hold it up. It could easily seat twelve, although only eight chairs were pushed under it.

The table was laden with food—a tempting selection of Indian dishes. The enticing aroma filled the air and yet was comforting and not overwhelming.

"One of the first things Rachel did was convert the old formal dining room into the second sitting room," Holmes said proudly. "She got rid of the fussy, formal table, chairs and serving board and found this enormous harvest table that she refinished."

"Is this that bloody awful table we drove to Wales to get and haul back?" asked Gabe.

"One and the same," said Holmes, beaming at Anne, who was admiring the table's design.

"If you like that, there are a bunch of things at the house you're going to love," said Sage, who had sold Gabe and Anne her restored home in the Outer Banks of North Carolina.

The buzzer on the gate sounded and after checking to ensure it was the takeaway delivery, Holmes let them in. He walked out to the driveway to pick up their order and brought it back in. The scent of Indian food wafted through the air.

"I hope you like curry. After smelling it all day, I had to have some."

While they ate, Eddy, Saoirse and Corinne caught the others up with all they'd figured out. After dinner, they wandered back into the sitting room to make further plans. The other four couples took up what Corinne was beginning to think of as their normal places. Gabe sprawled in a large chair, Anne ensconced on his lap. Roark took one end of the settee, Sage curled up next to him. Spense took the other end of the settee, Saoirse sitting in his lap. And Holmes took the other large chair, his legs spread, Rachel sitting between them at his feet, her head on his thigh as he stroked her hair. Corinne envied all of them as she went to share the smaller settee with Eddy. Their connections to each other were so palpable.

Before she could sit, though, Eddy took her by the hand and drew her into his lap. "Your place is here; being in each other's space is one of the best parts of a D/s relationship."

Corinne felt she was at one of those forks in the road that came along every so often in your life. She hadn't expected him to start her training, so to speak, until they were alone. Even then, she'd thought they might start tomorrow.

"Come, *chèrie*. I won't bite, at least not unless you want me to," he said seductively.

She settled herself in his lap. She could feel his cock harden beneath her and felt her body soften in a way it never had before. She wriggled around, trying to make herself comfortable in a way that wouldn't affect him so much, but the more she squirmed, the harder the large staff beneath her became.

His hand came up to stroke her spine. It wasn't overly sexual, but she found it soothing. She was glad of the loose-knit, baggy sweater as she was fairly sure no one could see her nipples stiffening. Eddy shifted beneath her, cradling her body with his and urging her head down on his shoulder.

"So, is there any way to prevent this thing from opening the portal?" asked Holmes.

"We haven't been able to figure one out. At this point, all we can do is be prepared when Big Ben strikes thirteen," answered Eddy.

"I think we ought to take turns sitting up until just after midnight so that if it strikes that thirteenth time, we can call everyone else and then meet at Trafalgar Square," suggested Rachel.

"Not everyone," admonished Holmes. "Spense will bring you, Anne and Sage back here until we know it's safe." Rachel started to protest but stopped when Holmes silenced her with a look. Corinne thought it was probably something they'd argued about before.

"Spense and Saoirse will stay at Trafalgar Square to give us cover and guard our six," he added, "Saoirse with a spell or two, Eddy with the bow. Gabe and Corinne will have swords, Roark will have the quarterstaff and I'll have the halberd. If all goes according to plan, we'll stop whatever's coming before it gets through and then Saoirse can seal the portal back up."

"What about the lions?" asked Anne.

"We're hoping to use them like supernatural war horses—only with claws and teeth," said Eddy. "We do need to see if Storm Shadow will accept me as its master."

"We can do that tomorrow," suggested Gabe. "I called Holcroft and arranged some private fight time for all of us in the morning at ten."

They continued to talk about their more immediate plans. And somehow, at some point as she'd cuddled in Eddy's lap, listening to the sound of his deep voice, and feeling safe and content, Corinne had fallen asleep. She barely recognized when he stood up with her in his arms and carried her up to his room. She started to protest, but Eddy spoke to her soothingly in French and she'd found it difficult to keep her eyes open.

Once inside his room, he set her on the bed, removing her boots before drawing her back up so he could push her leggings down, having her rest her hands on his shoulders as he helped her step out of them. He smiled, and she felt herself blush when he noticed she wore no panties. Holding her close enough that she could feel his erection between them, he grabbed the hem of her sweater and pulled it over her head.

"Maybe I could borrow one of your t-shirts or something. And I could go home," she said, lazily.

"*Non*. My sub sleeps naked at my side."

Oh god, if he unhooked her bra, not only would her boobs spill out, but he'd be able to see how aroused his mere presence made her. She supposed that was only fair, as he clearly had a strong reaction to her as well. He reached up and unhooked her bra. Corinne slipped it from her shoulders.

"*Mon Dieu*, you are beautiful," he whispered as he

raised his hand to trace the areola of her left breast before flicking her nipple.

"Not really, but it's nice of you to…" Corinne's sentence was cut off as Eddy's hand connected sharply with her naked ass. Heat and pain bloomed from the spot his hand had landed, making her gasp as much from surprise as discomfort.

"My sub is beautiful, and I find her more desirable than any other. No one gets to dispute that, not even her. Understand?"

"Shit, Eddy, that…" Again, the sentence turned to a gasp as he smacked her ass again.

"What did I tell you about cursing?"

"That I wasn't to do it. That may take some work…"

"Not to worry, *chèrie*, I will be here to help you with that."

"By swatting me when I do it?"

"*Non*. Tonight, I'm letting a lot of things slide. But come morning, you will learn to accept my authority and that breaking rules will get your pretty bottom spanked."

She really hated the way her body responded to him when he said that. Her nipples tightened even more, and her pussy softened and started to get wet—well, wetter than it had been before. She'd lied when she'd said she 'wouldn't mind' sleeping with him. Real-life Eddy was way sexier than book boyfriend Eddy, and she wanted him badly. He was standing so close she could feel the heat of his body reaching out to her like an electric arc.

Steadying her with one hand, he turned back the bed and helped her crawl in.

"I actually prefer this side of the bed," she said quietly.

"Then we will ensure at your flat, the bed is arranged so that you can have it. But I always sleep between you and the door."

"Is that like you holding doors for me and drawing me into your lap?"

"Yes, it's non-negotiable."

The bed was enormous and incredibly comfortable, and she tried not to be distracted by the thought of having sex with him in it, or in her bed, or anywhere at all. She felt incredibly out of her depth, as though she were swimming in uncharted water, yet with no desire to strike out for the safety of the shore. She could accept being the Sentinel of the Portal but having her own protector and other warriors with whom to battle evil sounded like a much better plan.

Eddy stripped down and when he, too, was naked, he slipped into bed beside her. He had folded their clothes and neatened the room before doing so, seemingly unconcerned that he was completely and beautifully naked. No man should look that good—well-defined muscles, not an ounce of flab on him, a great ass and a cock that seemed to defy gravity. She had to remind herself not to lick her lips or drool, but it was damned difficult to do.

"Just so you know, I'm clean and I've been on the pill for years."

He stretched out next to her, chuckling. "And you are the first woman I've been with on this side of the Veil. Sage always made sure that her men were clean. Just sleep, Corinne. The last few days have been hard on you. You need to rest. Don't worry about anything. We're together, and we'll take care of each other, *n'est-ce pas?*"

"Um, sure. Do you think a cold shower might help?"

"Would it help you? Yes, my cock is hard. It usually is when I'm close to you or even think about you. Tell me, Corinne, do your nipples always pebble up and your pussy begin to weep when you're with me?"

"My pussy... You don't know that" she accused.

"Oh, but I do. The sweet scent of your arousal calls to me. Do not lie to me again; that will get you spanked even quicker than cursing." She started to protest but he silenced her with a soft kiss, just a gentle brush of his lips against hers. "Go to sleep, *chèrie.* We've got a lot of work to do."

CHAPTER 18

*S*unlight filtered through the gauzy curtains that covered the windows. When her first inhale wasn't filled with Indian spices, Corinne remembered she no longer lived over the restaurant. She'd bought Rachel's old flat. As warm, smooth skin brushed against her, she realized she wasn't at her Charing Cross flat, either, but was lying in bed with Eddy at Holmes' Georgian townhouse.

Opening her eyes, she saw Eddy's strong arm draped across her middle, holding her close. Sometime after she'd fallen asleep, he'd spooned up against her. She lay still for a moment, enjoying the way it felt to be held by him. It felt good.

She tried convincing herself this was a bad idea, but she couldn't quite make any of her arguments ring true. In some ways they had only known each other for a few days, but in others she'd known him for years. Apparently, some ancient prophecy—although whether it was a curse or blessing remained unclear—had destined them to be together. Would it be so bad to have a protector? To have someone who would stand shoulder to shoulder with her to keep the city safe? God, she was beginning to feel a bit like Batman.

Eddy nuzzled her neck. "Did you sleep well?"

"I did, and you?" she said, starting to pull away.

"*Non*. You stay where I put you, remember?"

"Oh... Yes, Sir."

"Good girl," he purred in a lazy, sensual French accent. She was fairly sure the man could read a grocery list, and she'd get turned on. "And yes, I did. I rather like sleeping with you. Did you ever realize that in none of the books did Holmes, Roark or I sleep with anyone? We might have had sex, usually D/s sex, but never did we find the comfort of sleeping in our sweetheart's arms."

Corinne rolled her eyes and turned over to face him. Bad move! She could now feel his hard cock between them, and his hand stroked down her spine to cup her ass and pull her closer.

"You've got to stop that."

"Stop what? We've already discussed how my cock has a mind of its own. And the thing it wants most is to bury itself deep inside your wet pussy."

"Not that," she chuckled. "The mushy stuff."

"Ah. I am French—mushy stuff is part of the package."

This was going to be a problem. Every time she tried to establish some kind of boundary, he just ignored it and either made her laugh, swatted her bum or made her go weak at the knees. Maybe a good dose of reality would get through to him.

"I hope I didn't keep you awake. I've been told I snore," she said, studying him to see how he'd react.

Eddy laughed heartily. "You don't snore. You purr like the most precious kitten in the world."

"There you go again…"

She hadn't expected him to be able to swat her so hard while they were lying so close to each other. But she was wrong. Her butt smarted from where he'd just spanked her.

"I warned you about talking down about my sub. Next time will earn you five swats face-down over my knee, and I will make sure you feel each one."

Eddy's hand came up, cupping the nape of her neck; he held her still while he pressed his lips against hers. Arousal flashed through her system. His mouth was soft, seductive, persuasive, teasing hers until her lips parted and his tongue dipped into her mouth, sweeping through it and then sliding along her tongue, coaxing it to come and play with his.

His hand left her neck, tangling in her hair, tugging her head back so he could get a better angle on her mouth. His tongue invaded, capturing new ground and commanding her to yield without ever saying a word. Sweet, lovely Eddy's soft, playful kiss morphed in an instant to one that dominated, demanding her surrender. She couldn't seem to stop herself. Her arms wrapped around his neck, and she sighed as he pulled her closer and rolled to his back.

They lay together with her head resting on his chest, listening to the sure and steady beat of his heart. She allowed her hand to drift over the planes of his torso, exploring the musculature she found there. He was lean and every single line seemed to define and enhance his appearance; she wondered if he had any idea how gorgeous he was.

As her hand drifted below his waist, he caught it up and returned it to his pectoral muscles. "You ask before you play with me. And before you say it—no, I do not ask. Your body is mine to explore and enjoy."

She might have argued with him, but there was a knock on the door. "If you two want breakfast, you'd best get up," Holmes called through the door. "I told Roark and Gabe we'd meet them at Holcroft's."

"I don't want to," she said quietly to Eddy. "I don't want to be a superhero. I don't want any of it… well, except maybe you. I do want you."

"You're frightened and have every right to be," he soothed, caressing her. "There's nothing wrong with that. True courage comes when you are afraid and do what needs doing anyway. But you are no longer alone. I know this supernatural thing must feel strange. Your first taste of anything beyond this world were wild tales from the aunt your family told you was crazy. Then you find out you have a legacy that requires you to live in London waiting for Big Ben to do the impossible when the lions of Trafalgar Square come alive. And then, you learn your lover used to live in a book…"

"We're not technically lovers," she said, trying to recapture her equilibrium.

"Aren't we?" he asked. "I know that physically we have yet to have sex, but haven't you made love with me in your dreams and fantasies? I know I have to you. And have you ever felt as intimate with anyone as you do with me?"

Corinne didn't raise her head, but she smiled. "I'm glad you decided to come through the Veil to join your friends."

"I didn't come through the Veil for them. Most likely, I would have remained behind the Veil until it was no more. I came through the Veil for you."

And with that, Corinne decided that being afraid was okay and that she would do what needed doing so long as she could do it with the man at her side.

∼

Waking up with Corinne had been a revelation. It seemed to put the pieces of the puzzle into place. Well, not really, if he was honest with himself. There were still fragments missing... But the framework and main middle pieces were all in place. He and Corinne just needed to fill in the background and accents to complete the picture for good.

He hadn't lied when he'd told her he'd come through the Veil for her, and he'd known what he was talking about when he spoke of courage. The truth was, he'd remained behind the Veil even after he'd begun to develop feelings for her because he, too, had been afraid. He'd found the courage when he'd realized she could be in real danger, and he was unwilling to let his friends be the ones to protect her.

"I'm going to pull on some clothes and go downstairs. I want to talk to Holmes. Do you need me to have Rachel join you?" he asked, disengaging her warm body from his.

"Why do I need Rachel?"

"Because that bath is set up for a man to use, and you weren't planning to spend the night."

"True enough, but I'm glad I did."

He leaned down and kissed her softly, wishing he could take the time to explore her mouth with his before making slow, languid love to her.

"Me too. Don't be long. You need to have breakfast."

"I usually don't eat much."

He chuckled. "I know. That ends right now. I'll see you downstairs in a bit."

He left their room and caught Rachel just as she was going down the stairs.

"Good morning, Eddy. I take it you and Corinne slept well."

"We did. I wish it had been more than sleep, but she needed the rest."

Rachel smiled. "And like a good Dom, you're looking after her."

"You know how a good Dom treats his sub."

"Yes, I do."

"Could I ask you to see what she might need right now? I know we're going to swing by her place so she can change, but I don't know what she needs first thing in the morning."

"I'd be happy to, and I'm sorry I didn't think of it. I do know she likes coffee over tea, with lots of cream and a dab of honey, but then you probably already know that."

Eddy said nothing. Rachel had never been fond of the idea that Eddy was keeping tabs on Corinne. If she had any idea to what extent, she'd have had what Holmes referred to as a hissy fit. Eddy had to agree that Rachel in a temper was impressive. She was normally cool and collected, but when she lost her shit, it was kind of fun to watch.

He jogged down the stairs and joined Holmes in the kitchen. He was making breakfast. The aromas coming from the stove and oven were enticing. Eddy was glad Sage had written Holmes as an excellent, self-taught chef.

"Whatever that is, it smells incredible," said Eddy.

"Good morning to you too. You should learn to cook. There's something deeply satisfying about cooking a meal for your woman and feeding it to her. I made a breakfast casserole of eggs, sausage, potatoes and cheese. Then I thawed some frozen cinnamon roll dough and made a pull-apart."

"I can get behind the idea of you being a great chef, but there's something too feminine about baking for it to suit you."

He grinned, gesturing to the breakfast spread he was laying out for everyone. "You'd be surprised. I enjoy cooking. Rachel's a good cook as well and so we often do that together, but baking is relaxing. It's purely hedonistic and feeds the soul."

"You truly are the Renaissance man Sage created. Have you heard anything more about the guy who broke into Corinne's flat?" Eddy crossed his arms, leaning against the counter as they spoke.

"Other than he's dead, not much. What strikes me is that if this guy was looking for the weapons—specifically the sword and the bow—why? It's not something he'd be able to fence easily, and how would he know they were there in the first place?"

"Agreed. It seems to have been too specific for just a random burglary, and when you watch the tape, he's clearly looking for something specific. Do you think it's the weapons he was after?"

"In all honesty," said Holmes, "it's the only thing of real value she has. Hiding the bow and sword in that blanket chest under a false bottom was pretty clever. He left the quarterstaff and the halberd alone. I don't think he knew what they were or their significance."

"So, you think someone hired him to search for Storm Shadow and Galatine."

"Yes. And what's more, I think when he didn't get them, whoever hired him decided he was too much of a loose end and killed him." Holmes popped a bite of cinnamon roll into his mouth, then pointed to Eddy's chest.

"You, my friend, need to make time for Corinne. She needs to be your priority. I can get one of our tech guys to see what he can do. Keep in mind that being here isn't like the other side. You get hungry, you need rest, and you'll find you really need to get laid."

"I plan to be working on the last one later today. I used to scoff at you when you said that making love to your wife was one of your great joys, but so was sleeping with her in your arms and waking up next to her. I thought that was a line of romantic bullshit."

Holmes snorted. "I thought you French guys were all about romantic bullshit."

Eddy shrugged lightly. "We are, but we are also

eminently practical and acknowledge that sex is a profound need, one not to be underrated. But I bow to your expertise. There was something incredibly special about waking up spooned with Corinne."

"And the other? The profound need?"

Eddy laughed. "I mean to have that need well seen to within short order."

CHAPTER 19

Holmes drove Eddy and Corinne back to her flat so she could retrieve the bow and the sword. Roark and Gabe were going to meet them at Holcroft's fighting salon.

"The first thing we have to know is if Storm Shadow will accept Eddy as its master," said Corinne. "Holmes, I think you, Roark and Gabe should work with Holcroft. Eddy and I will go over to the archery range to try out Storm Shadow."

Eddy nodded. "Sounds good. I don't know about anyone else, but I'm inclined to keep anyone outside of our tight-knit little group in the dark about what's going on and what we're up to."

"I spoke with Spense," said Holmes. "And we're good on that. He's scheduled Corinne to be on vacation for a week after the time she'd already requested. He said you have way too much vacation just sitting there. He also said Saoirse has her nose buried in her spell books. She doesn't know that the spell she used at the Tower is big enough and strong enough to cover this."

When they entered the warehouse that housed Holcroft's fighting salon, the fight master himself wasn't there, but one of his proteges—a stuntman who did quite a bit of work in television and movies—greeted them and agreed to work with Holmes, Watson and Roark.

"Are you just going to watch?" asked the stuntman.

"No, my boyfriend is also an excellent archer, and we thought we'd go over to the range, but I'd also like to get in some sword practice."

"An excellent plan. Holcroft apologized for not being here, but he hadn't been expecting you…"

"That's fine, Max. We were just having dinner last night and thought it might be a fun thing to do."

Corinne left Holmes, Watson and Roark in Max's capable hands and walked with Eddy toward the archery range. Eddy carried both cases—one under his arm and one by its handle—and took her by the hand. Corinne gave him a brief tour.

"You know, your Holcroft is an interesting character," said Eddy when they were at a safe distance from the group and could talk out of Max's earshot.

"How so?"

"He has impeccable credentials, but his background and history are a bit murky. Nothing to really raise any alarms, but a bit vague and unspecific."

"He's been very kind to me. He was the only other person at my aunt's funeral and seemed to have genuinely cared for her."

They were the only people at the warehouse aside from Max. When they got to the area reserved for archery, Eddy released her hand and placed the case containing Storm Shadow on top of Galatine's case. Reverently, he opened it and trailed his hand down the limbs of the bow in what almost looked like a lover's caress.

"She is very beautiful. Let's hope she sees me as friend and not foe," said Eddy.

"You think the bow is a she?"

"But of course. She is beautiful, strong, graceful and must yield to her master's hand in order to be her best—very feminine traits. Galatine, and all other swords, are more masculine—strong, far more forceful in how they kill."

"How will you know if Storm Shadow accepts you?"

"I'll be alive," he said, reaching for the bow.

Corinne stayed his hand. "Excuse me? Are you telling me that if you try to use the bow and she rejects you, you could die? Does that mean my aunt gave me a weapon that might have killed me?"

"Yes and no. In the case of your aunt giving her to you, that was an inheritance. This bow has been passed down through your family for centuries. There was never any chance that she would reject you. You are your aunt's successor. But me? To her, I am an interloper. As far as she knows I could have stolen her or be trying to harm you."

"Are you saying the bow is sentient?"

"Not in the way you think of it. Does she have the ability to think and act independently? No. But she was blessed with an innate sense of who she belongs to and will not betray that sacred trust."

Corinne shook her head. "I don't like the idea of you risking your life just to use Storm Shadow. Can't you use another bow?"

"No. Only Storm Shadow or one of her sister bows has the range and power we need for the coming fight. It will be all right, *mon amour*."

Corinne refused to let go of his hand. "No. You just escaped the book… I just found you in this reality. I don't want to lose you."

"Courage," he whispered. Then he picked up the bow and string, standing up as he did so. "So far, so good. There are stories of her burning the hands of those she was rejecting."

Eddy took Storm Shadow firmly in hand and strung the bow. Corinne was impressed by the speed and ease with which he did so, as if he was a natural to it. She leaned down, picking up the quiver and handing him an arrow.

"She takes a bit of pulling."

"Like her mistress, she enjoys a show of strength," he teased.

Corinne rolled her eyes, feeling a bit better about whether or not Storm Shadow would accept Eddy. He took the arrow and notched it onto the bowstring. Gripping the string with his index, middle and ring fingers, placing the arrow between the first two, Eddy raised the bow into position, resting the arrow on his closed fist, holding it firmly as he pulled back on the bowstring. He took aim and then relaxed the fingers on the bowstring, letting it slip from his grip and fire the arrow. She watched as it struck dead center in the target.

Eddy lowered the bow and wrapped his other arm around her. Lowering his mouth to hers, he slid his tongue past her teeth—tasting, exploring and claiming as he did so. She felt a difference in the way Eddy kissed her now. Even the most casual brushing of his lips across hers made arousal bloom and wildfire race through her body. She'd never enjoyed kissing before; it had seemed embarrassing, awkward and sometimes downright messy. But kissing Eddy was another thing altogether. She could kiss him endlessly, allowing a lazy, mutual exploration of each other.

When he let her come up for air, she smiled. "You're still breathing, and that thing throbbing between us seems to be alive… so I guess that means she's accepted you."

"I think, perhaps, it is because she knows that you,

too, have acknowledged your master."

Eddy loosed three more arrows into three separate targets; each struck squarely in the center of the bullseye. He unstrung the bow before wiping it down and putting it gently back in its case. While he did so, Corinne collected the arrows, wiped down the tips and replaced them in the quiver. Eddy closed the case, picked up the bow and the sword, took Corinne by the hand and led her back to join their friends.

Holmes and Roark were sparring—halberd against quarterstaff. Both men fought far more adeptly than Corinne had thought they would. Both had progressed past the point where they would be easily disarmed by rapping the weapon against the opponent's fingers. Which was good, because after all, they had no way of knowing if their opponents would even have fingers. Roark seemed to favor the strike, using the length of the quarterstaff, while Holmes preferred to stab at his opponent, which made sense as the halberd did have a pointy end. Corinne watched with fascination as two thoroughly modern men sparred with weapons from an age long ago.

"Gentlemen," said Max, "I'm amazed at your skill and physical prowess. We have showers in the back, but you might want to watch this. Watson here tells me he's a good swordsman. I've sparred with Corinne, and she is exceptional. It's as if the sword is merely an extension of her hand."

Corinne opened the case and drew out Galatine.

From the moment she picked it up, it was as if an electrical charge raced up her arm and suffused her system, giving her fresh strength. It had never done that before during her sparring matches, and as she glanced at Gabe, she could tell that he, too, was feeling something similar from his own blade, Courechouse.

Taking their places on the thick rubber matted area. Crossing swords, she said in an undertone to Gabe, "I take it that was new to you as well."

"Yes. Weird, not exactly painful, but different."

As fighters, Gabe and Corinne were fairly evenly matched. Corinne had the edge on training and experience, but Gabe outmatched her for strength and endurance. Time and again the two swords clanged and slid. It seemed somehow as though sparks should fly. The combatants fought with a singular determination to best one another—both trying to prove their mettle to those with whom they would face something from another dimension.

The hanging pendant lamps flashed their light on the glinting steel as each tried to best the other, but it was a balanced fight with as much give as there was take. The song of the broadswords rattled and reverberated throughout the warehouse. Her shoulders ached. She'd never fought for this long with such a skilled opponent. Finally, Max called a halt.

"In any competition fight, this would be considered a draw," he announced. "I suggest all of you drink some water and go hit the showers." Max tossed each of them a bottle. "Corinne, you can show them to the showers, right?"

"Absolutely. Gentlemen, if you'll follow me."

She guided them through the large, open space, sending the others into the men's locker room. Because she worked out with Holcroft so often and paid to be able to use the space at any time, Corinne had one of the few private lockers in the women's area. She was shocked when she rounded the corner and discovered her lock had been cut off. When she opened the door, some of her things tumbled out. Someone had broken into her locker and gone through her things. She wondered if it was the same person who had burgled her old flat. She knew there were security cameras in place; perhaps Eddy could make his way through the footage and confirm whether or not it had been the same man.

This was the second time in a week where she'd felt violated. It was irrational, but something about this was even worse than having someone break into her home. The fight salon had always been her safe place; the place few even knew about, much less understood. She wiped away the tears that wanted to form.

Walking to the shower, she turned on the hot water and allowed it to beat down on her. Certain no one could hear her, she allowed herself the luxury of crying. It had been a long time since she'd indulged herself in that. The first inkling she had that Eddy had joined her was when muscular arms enfolded her into his embrace as he hauled her up against his body. It didn't even surprise her; she felt relieved he'd come to find her.

"What is it, sweetheart?" he whispered.

"Someone broke into my locker. They went through my things. It wasn't just random or bad luck at my old place, was it? Who is this guy, and what does he want from me?"

"I'll look through the security camera feed. It was most likely the same guy, but you don't need to be afraid," he reassured her.

"Why not?" she said, wiping away angry, frightened tears. "I'm supposed to be facing some kind of demon from another dimension, but at least I have you guys to back me up. Now, I'm the target of some guy who just breaks into my places and tries to steal from me."

"You are no longer alone. I suspect the same man broke into both places—it's pretty obvious he was looking for Galatine and Storm Shadow, which he didn't find. You have no need to fear him because he was found murdered, probably by the same person who hired him."

She looked up at him, her hair and bedraggled, wet mess and tears making tracks down her face. "If that's your way of trying to comfort me, it isn't working."

"Yes, it is," he said, cupping her face and wiping away her tears with his thumbs. "You don't need to worry about him. And until this is done, I will be with you at all times, keeping you safe."

"That's not practical."

"Perhaps not, but I am the Protector and I take my job very seriously."

Cradled against his chest, Corinne allowed the tears to come and cleanse her soul in the same way the heat and steam of the shower was removing the sweat and exhaustion of her fight with Gabe. The heat and intimacy of standing naked in Eddy's arms comforted and strengthened her in a way that nothing else ever had. She felt closer to him than she'd ever felt to anyone. His hands moved over body, soothing her as they went. His cock pressed hard against her body, but he ignored it.

As if reading her mind, he said, "It will wait."

She sagged against him, resting her head on his chest with her arms wrapped around his waist. He picked up the shower sponge from her caddy and, squeezing gel onto it, began to wash her body. She moaned as she stirred and tried to pull away.

"I can do it myself," she murmured dreamily.

"Yes, but I want to do it. Those without a clue think it is only the sub who serves the Dom, but it isn't true. A lot of Doms give it another label—aftercare, worship—but it's really the same thing."

"That's nice," she purred as she leaned against him.

He continued to soap up each area of her body and then ensured it was washed clean. He interspersed long strokes with the sponge with kisses he trailed behind them as the suds were rinsed away. His hands slid down between her legs, glancing over her clit back to the opening of her core. She'd never been one for physical affection outside the bedroom and had never wanted a man in her shower, but she was beginning to think that the idea of her body being at his beck and call might not be such a bad thing.

Once she was clean, he made short work of his own shower before scooping her up in his arms and walking to where the towels were kept. He took his time drying her off, blotting away the excess water, before lightly rubbing it dry. He ran the towel over every inch of her body, following behind with kisses and sweet caresses. Corinne had never done drugs, but she was beginning to understand how it must feel if someone did them and their appeal to others. Eddy was bringing her to bliss as he cared for her. He blotted her hair and then pulled it back, braiding it lightly and securing it with one of the small scrunchies she kept in her caddy.

After they'd dressed, they made order of her locker and then Eddy extended his hand.

"Come on, sweetheart, let's go join the others."

CHAPTER 20

Once they were in the car and had endured the teasing of their friends as to how long it had taken them to shower and rejoin them, Eddy relayed the fact that Corinne's locker had been broken into.

"I'm going to go through the security camera footage and confirm that it was the same man," said Eddy.

"But why is he coming after me now?" asked Corinne.

Eddy wrapped his arm around her. "Most likely because whoever it is knows what's coming and is trying to weaken you. Killing the man who broke into your place was just his or her way of tying up loose ends."

"I just wish we knew when it was coming," she said.

"We must be close, or no one would be worried about you and the threat you pose to them. Keep in mind," drawled Holmes, "in some ways it's kind of a compliment."

"I'd rather they send flowers," she groused as she snuggled into Eddy.

Holmes' mobile rang and he answered, putting it on speaker.

"Sweetheart, don't drop off Eddy and Corinne. Roark and Gabe are headed here, and the rest of the gang has already arrived," said Rachel.

"What's happened?"

"Someone's broken into everyone's homes. I called Landry and let him know. He said that was a bit too coincidental—our closest friends all being broken into. He wanted to let you know he'd send a team to each place. They've stopped by to get keys. I gave them my copy to Corinne's."

"Is everyone all right? Are you?" asked Holmes.

"Yes, more annoyed than scared, but Spense and Saoirse thought it might not be a bad idea to all gather together. We have the room, so Camp Scary Stuff is back in session."

Holmes chuckled. "Well, I can think of worse things. Do you need me to pick anything up?"

"No, we're all stocked up and I've got everyone assigned to their rooms. See you soon."

No sooner had the call ended with Rachel than Eddy's mobile rang. Eddy answered and he, too, hit the speaker function. "Gabe? I take it you've heard we're all headed to Holmes' place. They broke into Corinne's locker at Holcroft's."

"Sounds like they're getting desperate," said Gabe. "I think we ought to split our forces this evening, make a big show of leaving the townhouse to go out to dinner. Then while you and Spense entertain the girls, Holmes, Roark and I will see if they try and take advantage of what they believe to be an empty townhouse."

"Saoirse and I should be with you," said Corinne.

"That's not happening," said Eddy.

Before he could continue, Holmes interrupted. "He's right, Corinne. In all honesty, we need to ensure you and Eddy are kept the safest. In fact, I think it should be just Roark and me. If something goes sideways at the townhouse, then you, Eddy and Gabe are still our best shot at stopping this thing."

"Then we're set. Let's all meet at the townhouse, take a little time to decompress and then put our plan in action."

Once everyone had assembled at the townhouse, Eddy grabbed his computer, kissed Corinne and then went to work hacking Holcroft's system to review the security footage. Corinne watched Eddy as he ate with distraction, his focus on the screen in front of him.

"Yes!" he cried in triumph. "Here he is. Same guy or his evil *doppelgänger*."

"At least we know he won't be coming to bother us, but it then begs the question, who broke in today?"

"That's where it gets a bit spooky... I checked everyone's security cameras. I can see the break-ins and I can see things being moved, but there is no image as to who or what is moving items around. Now, there is technology that would allow them to do that, but it's expensive as hell and would have required that they hack your systems..."

"Let me guess," said Holmes, "you can't find any evidence of that, right?"

"Correct."

After dinner, all of the couples retreated to their own rooms.

"You all right, *chèrie*?" Eddy asked as he closed the door behind them.

"Not really, but I will be. I'm so glad I'm not going through this by myself, but I really feel Saoirse and I should be here with Holmes and Roark, especially given what you saw—or rather, didn't see."

"I understand, but sometimes the best and hardest thing to do is to sit and wait on the sidelines. As much as I don't like it either, I think Holmes' reasoning is sound."

"I do too, but that doesn't mean I have to like it."

He held her close, stroking her hair. "No, sweetheart, it doesn't. But now, it's time to rest. Why don't you get naked and crawl into bed?"

"Are you going to join me?" she teased, her body coming alight with desire.

She did as he asked and waited for him to undress. Instead of doing so, he merely looked down at her.

"You've acclimated very quickly to being my sub," he started.

That took her aback, and she tried hard not to recoil. "I guess I have more submissive qualities than I thought." She started to roll away from him. "I can ask Rachel to find me another room."

"Another room? What the hell are you talking about?"

"If you've changed your mind, I get it. You're like some French god and gift to womankind, while I'm just..."

"Finish that and you'll regret it," he warned. He shook his head. "*Merde.* I was trying to play the gentleman. I don't want you to feel forced into a relationship or to have sex with me."

He tore open his shirt, flinging it across the room as he toed out of his shoes and opened the fly to his jeans. Once more, his glorious cock stood at rigid attention. All doubts about whether he found her attractive fled.

"Sorry," she said sheepishly.

"As you should be," he said, disposing of his jeans and joining her on the bed. "Corinne, you have to understand I don't just want you for right now. I don't want to have some fling, fight the bad guys and then ride off into the sunset."

She nodded. "Can I touch you?"

"Good girl," he purred. "And yes, you may touch me anywhere you like until we leave our bed."

She traced the stubble along his jawline with her finger, studying his face and the ways his pupils dilated. She hadn't been joking. He really was gorgeous. Eddy studied her as well, not so much as moving a muscle. Corinne leaned over and lightly ran her lips over the skin of his cheek and then back down to trace where her fingers had gone. She bypassed his mouth, working back up the other side of his jaw, to his other cheek and then pressed a kiss to each eye.

"You do know you're going to kill me, don't you?" he said in a strained voice.

"But I think not a bad way to die."

He chuckled. "*Merde*. Not even twenty-four hours in, and already you are showing your bratty side."

Corinne pulled back. "Is that a bad thing?" she asked.

"*Non*. It is a very good thing, but keep in mind, brats tend to get spanked far more often than proper subs, and *non*, I have never really enjoyed proper subs."

Feeling her confidence grow, she allowed her mouth to hover over his just for a moment before pressing her lips to his warm, soft, sensual lips. She knew he was exercising great control and she thought she should take advantage of it. As she deepened the kiss, she let her hand drift down his torso, trailing down his washboard abs until she could wrap her fist around the main stalk of his desire. Eddy shifted to give her better access.

"*Allez*," he groaned.

She kissed him again as she grasped him, enjoying the way he shivered beneath her touch. Her nipples had already beaded in response to him being near, but now her pussy was getting wetter and softening, beginning to pulse with need. She emboldened her kiss, letting her tongue enter his mouth and play with his. Eddy responded in kind but made no move to rush her.

"Corinne, please, give over to me. Another day I will let you play all you want, but let me lead this first time," he said, his fist coming up to tangle in her hair.

She let her smile answer for her, and the prize that had laid out before her became a dominant male. He reached out to touch her breast, tracing her areola with his finger before finding her nipple and giving it a sharp pinch and then a tug. Her sudden inhalation of air became a moan as he enveloped both the darkened center of her breast and its pebbled peak in his mouth, swirling his tongue all around. Nothing had ever felt better. Nothing.

The shock of the brief, intense pain was replaced quickly by the warmth and soothing quality of his mouth. It was as if both pain and pleasure had merged into one and sent a bolt of electricity surging through her body. Her pussy went from pulsing to throbbing in the space of a heartbeat. Want and need surged through her veins as he nudged her onto her back.

~

The moment she surrendered to him, he rolled over her, spreading her legs and making a place for himself. He looked into her eyes and felt his soul meld with her. She was the single most beautiful, sensual creature he had ever encountered—and no demon from another dimension was going to steal her away from him.

Kissing his way down from her navel to her sex, he nipped and sucked along the way. Each time she squirmed, but not once did she try to get away. A dark, sultry quality deepened the color of her eyes, and she accepted his dominance and offered him the gift of her submission—a gift he meant to cherish.

He moved down until he reached her clit. He flicked it with his tongue before giving it a brief suck and then an even quicker nip. She writhed beneath him, but he had no intention of letting her squirm away. He could feel her heat and smell her arousal. God, he loved the way she smelled, and he was willing to bet she tasted even better.

Eddy drew himself up on his knees, staring down

at her, reveling in the sight of her swollen, wet sex. His cock bobbed in anticipation, reminding him he could eat his fill of her later. Right now, all it wanted was to get deep inside her. Eddy ignored it, preferring to ensure that he didn't rush and let this first time be special.

As if to spit in his eye, his cock dripped pre-cum on her belly. Scooping it up with his finger, he rubbed it into her clit. There would come a day when he came all over her, marking her as his, but this time, he meant to fill her pussy as he emptied himself into her.

"Shit, Eddy, I'm dying here."

His wicked grin was the only indication she had at what was about to come.

"I believe I've warned you more than once about cursing."

He flipped her over onto her belly and ran his hand over her ass, while using the other hand to pin her into place. He smacked her ass hard, holding the heat and sting into her flesh. She gasped but didn't try to get away or swear at him again. He spanked her twice more, each time letting the full impact settle into her. She didn't make a sound. Eddy delivered the last two, again letting the heat and sting making a lasting impression and turning pain to arousal.

"Good girl. You handled that well. I'm proud of you," he said, running his hand between her legs to stroke and explore her glistening labia.

He stroked the petals of her sex, his cock throbbing in anticipation. He could hear, feel and smell her arousal—it radiated off her body like heat waves rolling up from the desert floor. He'd thought he'd been hard thinking about her, watching her, or being close to her, but it was nothing compared to the knowledge that before the afternoon was over, he'd have been deep inside her, emptying his balls to fill up her pussy so that when they went to dinner, he'd know she was full of his cum.

Eddy flipped her to her back and settled back between her legs, running his tongue in circles around her clit before he licked down to the opening of her core, making her squirm. He was sure she was feeling the residual heat from her abbreviated spanking, but he'd make that memory fade. He took a long, deep swipe with his tongue, savoring her taste as he licked and sucked every delightful, secret, hidden place. If he'd thought she was hot before, it was nothing compared to the inferno that was threatening to engulf her completely. Her body was racing toward the abyss. He plunged his tongue deep, spearing her pussy. Fresh arousal coated his tongue. She was ready, and so by God was he.

His throbbing cock seemed to grow even harder in anticipation. It would have its prize and didn't much care what anyone thought about it. He crawled up her body, his dick pounding and aimed at her core. She would sheathe his sword and he would make her scream with pleasure as she did so. She'd most likely be sore when he got done, but he didn't care. But he should care because it would be a bad thing if demons were released into the world because of how hard he fucked her.

When his cock was poised at her entrance, he surged in, her wet heat clamping down as she came, but he continued to sink to her depths. He thrust in partway, drew back and then forward again. She was tight, he was large, but her pussy would adjust and learn to accommodate his size.

"Eddy," she wailed with intense pleasure as he continued to push in.

Over and over he surged in, dragged himself backward and then tunneled inside again. He groaned, giving voice to both satisfaction and need. Nothing had ever felt as exquisite as her pussy contracting all up and down his length. He reached under her, taking the globes of her ass in his hands, holding her steady as he buried himself up to his balls.

He ground himself against her clit, making her cry out in a little mini-orgasm. He dragged himself almost all the way out and then thrust in again, hard. He slid back and surged in, finding a rhythm that made her cry out, wrapping her arms around him, intertwining her legs with his, and trying desperately to undulate her hips, but he held her still. She needed to learn from the first that he would lead, she would follow; he would dominate, and she would submit.

Eddy began pounding into her, harder and harder with each thrust. Her body stiffened in anticipation; her nails raked his back and he responded with a low, guttural sound that spoke to the deepest part of his soul. Her pussy was trying to strangle his cock, and nothing had ever felt so good. Eddy had no words for the depths of pleasure that this one woman could and would give him.

Short, sharp strokes hammered her pussy until finally he drove deep, emptying himself inside her. He gave her everything he had. No demon would take her away from him. He would blow open the gates to Hell itself if he had to, in order to keep her with him. As he filled her, a deep peace and satisfaction washed over him. He nuzzled her neck and held her close as he rolled to his back, taking her with him.

He looked into her eyes—deep and primal satiation filled them. "Wow, oh wow," she said before laying her head on his chest.

CHAPTER 21

Corinne wasn't sure when she'd fallen asleep or when Eddy had slipped away from her body. All she knew was that when she woke, the afternoon had deepened, and she felt his loss. Rolling over, she saw a white rose that looked as though it had been dipped in blood. There was a note propped up on it, telling her to join them downstairs in the sitting room when she was able to. *What the hell does he mean by that?*

She rolled up off the bed, swinging her legs over the side and winced. It was a toss-up as to whether her pussy or her backside was more sore. The really insane thing was, she couldn't wait for either of those experiences to happen again. How sick was it that a spanking had turned her on the way it had? She was beginning to understand the allure of D/s.

Carefully, she made her way into the bath and

cleaned up. She slipped on her clothes and slipped out of their room, meeting Rachel and Sage at the top of the stairs.

As they started down, Sage said, "Oh dear, you look like I feel."

Corinne laughed. "Did you have to write him that well-hung and enthusiastic?"

Sage laughed with her, as did Rachel, who said, "At least you knew what to expect… I'd never read the books."

Once they'd descended the staircase, they joined the others.

"So the plan is Roark, Holmes and Spense will remain here at the townhouse. Gabe and Eddy will take the ladies out to dinner. We'll take three SUVs, one of which will contain those who will stay behind," said Eddy.

"I can see taking Corinne with you, but I should be here. Arguably I have the most experience in dealing with supernatural boogeymen."

"And like Corinne, if you aren't available to keep what happens that night away from prying eyes, the whole world might turn upside-down and some power-hungry idiot might decide a demon army is the ticket to success."

Crossing her arms, Rachel said, "I won't go. It's my home too, and I'm not integral to the fight. I wouldn't be a great loss."

"You would to me," said Holmes. "And you'll

agree to behave, or I'll send you with Gabe and Eddy in handcuffs with a brightly colored backside."

"Don't start, Sage," warned Roark. "You're going too. Besides, I don't think the big battle is tonight, but I do think we might have visitors… visitors who might be able to give us information we need."

In the end, every argument made by one of the women was trounced into the ground by the men in their lives. Grumbling about being involved with chauvinistic bastards, they all went out to the SUVs and made a great show of leaving the townhouse empty. Roark, Holmes and Spense would double back and reenter the mansion using a hidden entrance into a tunnel that ran most of the length of the alley.

Gabe was driving the SUV with Anne and Rachel, while Eddy had Corinne, Saoirse and Sage with him. They'd made reservations for a restaurant outside the city when Eddy had discovered the phone was tapped. He'd been able to narrow and isolate the band so they could cherry-pick the information the other side heard.

They parked and headed into the restaurant. After they'd ordered and their appetizers had been served, Saoirse managed to spill Marinara sauce in her lap.

"Damn, this is silk," she said, angrily dabbing at the stain. "Corinne, you're a concierge. Spense always knows the best ways to treat these things so they don't become permanent. Can you help me?"

"Sure thing," said Corinne, leaving the table with

the wily Irish witch. Once they rounded the corner to head down the hall to the loo and a back exit, Corinne looked at Saoirse. "We aren't really going to work on getting a stain out… are we?"

"I don't know about your part of *we*, but my part of *we* sure as hell isn't. The boys don't know it, but I swiped an extra set of keys. I'm not sure which SUV it'll work on, but I didn't think it really mattered. I think we should be there if something shows up."

"Me too. I think if it's supernatural, we step in to help. Otherwise, we can just fade into the background."

Just outside the restaurant, Saoirse turned to her. "Look, you're new to all this D/s stuff. Right, wrong or indifferent, you and I are going to be in a whole lot of trouble, and you should know we're going to get spanked. Spense and Eddy are going to be pissed on a myriad of levels, including our blatant disrespect for defying them in front of their friends."

"I consider myself forewarned and will not hold you responsible for any consequences that might get inflicted on me."

Saoirse hit the unlock button on the SUVs and then headed for the one whose doors it didn't unlock.

"I thought it was the other one," Corinne said.

"It is," said Saoirse, pulling a small dagger from a strap hidden high on her thigh and plunging it into one of the tires. "That ought to slow them down."

They were pulling out of the driveway when Eddy

and Gabe came barreling out of the restaurant, shouting after them as they drove away. Once they were back in the city, Saoirse drove them to Chelsea and pulled down the alley behind Holmes' townhouse.

When she drove past the back gate, Corinne swiveled her head around "What did you see?"

"The gate had been unlocked and opened. They pushed it almost shut, but not enough for it to relock. Call the boys and tell them it's about to go down."

"No thanks. I'm going to text Spense. He'll have his phone on vibrate; then I'll call Anne."

Anne answered on the first ring. "You are in so much trouble."

"That's fine and dandy, but someone has gone in the back way."

She looked down, and there was a succinct reply from Spense's phone:

WE HAVE THEM BUT ARE WILLING TO MAKE A DEAL

"You know we can't go in there," said Saoirse. "It's a trap."

"I'm sure it is, but I can't not go in. Holmes put the weapons in a hidden safe in what used to be a priest hole. Whoever it is will never find it, and Holmes will never give them what they need."

"So we have nothing to trade."

Corinne unbuckled her seat belt, twisted around and opened the case containing *Courechouse*.

"I wouldn't," said Saoirse. "That thing packs a nasty punch."

"I'm under no illusion that it would prefer to have Gabe here, but I'm hoping it'll recognize I have one of the other swords and let me try to save our friends."

Hoping she was right, she reached into the case and picked up the sword by its hilt. There was a nasty little charge of that same electrical surge she'd felt earlier in the day, but not much worse.

"I think we'll be okay. You take the SUV and go down to the alley entrance and direct them down this way."

"I don't think you should go alone."

"And I don't think we should risk both of us. I may wield Galatine and the lions, but you have magick. We don't stand a chance against whatever's coming if both of us fall this night."

"Not the front or back gate. Most likely they'll be waiting or at least watching. There's a hidden entrance down here. Once you get to the tunnel, it'll lead you straight to the townhouse's pantry. That's your best bet for getting in."

Corinne nodded and when Saoirse stopped the SUV, Corinne slipped out, lifting the cover to the entrance and climbing down the ladder into the dark.

She ran along the tunnel, feeling her way with her hand against the damp wall, until she came to the ladder that would lead her up into the townhouse. Slowly she climbed up, peeking through a small hole to ensure no one was in the pantry. She let herself in and then tried to quiet her breathing so she could hear.

"Has she replied?" said a voice that sounded all too familiar.

"Nothing yet, my lady. Can't you find the damn things without their help?" said a male voice.

"If I could do that, I wouldn't need you idiots, now would I?" the woman said in a scathing tone, immediately before there was a crackle of lightning. "Care to be next?"

Corinne crept out, forcing fear and tension from her body. Her fear would serve no one. What was it Eddy had said? Courage was doing what needed doing, even when you were afraid. She had a job to do—secure the freedom of her friends regardless of the cost. She moved quietly and efficiently. At this moment, silence was her only ally.

She made her way down the back hallway until she could see into the sitting room. The woman was standing with her back to her, as was her thug. All three men—Holmes, Roark and Spense—were tied together sitting on the couch. She couldn't see a gun.

All three men spotted her, but not one of them

betrayed it with their expressions. She curled back around the corner out of sight and made a tiny scratching noise.

"What was that?" said the thug.

"Probably nothing, but go see," replied the woman who had once been her aunt's caregiver. Corinne had a few questions to ask her about her aunt's rapid decline.

The thug came around the corner, but before he could sound the alarm, Corinne had swung the sword and removed his head, which fell with a thud and a lot of blood before rolling back into the sitting room.

"Corinne? Come in, my dear. We have much to discuss."

Straightening her shoulders, Corinne walked into the room, the sword held at the ready.

"You don't look surprised to see me," said Delores.

"I recover quickly when that last little piece falls into place. How could you?"

"Your aunt wouldn't give me what I needed to appease my mistress."

"Who might that be?" asked Corinne.

"She who bore the son of the king that was and will be again,"

Delores' laugh bordered on the maniacal and she directed her wand toward Corinne, releasing its power. Instinctively, Corinne brought the sword up in front of her, deflecting the deadly bolt into a large ornate mirror and shattering it.

"Galatine…" whispered Delores, the first notes of concern entering her voice.

"Nope, but you're close. I suggest you get out of here before the sword's true master shows up."

"I fear no man," said Delores, in a tone that indicated just the opposite.

Delores fired off another round and Corinne was able to repel it with the same deft counter measures, this time destroying what she was sure was a valuable vase. Corinne was more prepared for the third salvo as she and Delores circled each other. Instead of redirecting the lightning wildly, Corinne was able to give it more aim and specific direction, landing it at Delores' feet and causing her to jump back.

"Bitch," screeched Delores, clearly surprised at Corinne's deft mastery of the blade.

Speaking in a language Corinne had never heard, Delores released another discharge from her wand. Growing more confident in her ability to wield Courechouse, Corinne advanced on Delores, deflecting the deadly lightning as Delores fired at her repeatedly. Delores was able to avoid being hit and aimed the wand again. This time, Corinne stepped in its direction, lifting the blade and angling it so that the bolt of energy seemed to bounce off the gleaming sword and reflect it back to its sender.

Delores screamed as the lightning ran up the wand to envelop her in an electrical storm of sparks and crackling energy. It only lasted a moment until Delores was gone, vaporized by the magick that she had ultimately unleashed upon herself.

"Are there any others?" Corinne asked as she rushed forward, using the keen blade to cut the rope from the three men.

"No. There were only three, and she killed one right before you got here," said Roark.

"Spense, you might want to give Saoirse the all-clear. I suspect the rest of them are headed back." She looked down at the shirt she'd been wearing, which was now soaked in blood. "I think I'd like to take a shower." She wiped the blood from the blade of the sword, setting it inside the umbrella holder by the front door. "You should tell Gabe that's where it is. I wouldn't try picking it up. It can give a rather nasty shock."

She turned, feeling like a zombie as she trudged up the stairs. She entered the room she shared with Eddy. As weird as it was, she hoped he'd spank her. She knew she had disappointed him by disobeying, but at the time, she hadn't seen any other way to do it. Of course, she knew that was wrong. She could have made Eddy and Gabe see that she and Saoirse were right, but that time was past.

Corinne made her way into the bedroom she shared with Eddy and stripped out of her clothes.

The shirt, she wadded up and put in a trash bag; the rest, she put in the laundry hamper. She entered the bath and turned on the shower. Opening the glass door, she stepped in to allow the heat and steam to envelop her completely.

CHAPTER 22

*C*orinne stepped under the hot, pelting water. It felt wonderful. Downstairs she'd felt perfect, strong and in control. Severing the thug's head from his body hadn't bothered her in the least. Killing her aunt's former caregiver had seemed like the thing to do at the time. It was only now when she was once again alone that she realized the consequences for what she'd done might be more far reaching than she'd bargained for. She wished Eddy had been here—not to wield the sword or even protect her, but to hold her in his arms and tell her everything would be all right.

When she finished washing herself clean, she stepped out of the shower to find Eddy leaned against the vanity.

"Are you all right?" he asked with no intonation to give her a clue as to how he was feeling.

"I'm not hurt."

"That's not what I asked. Are you all right?"

"Yes. No. I don't know."

He reached out to grasp her hand and drag her into his body.

"I'm going to get you all wet."

"I don't care," he said, wrapping her in his strong embrace. "You scared the shit out of me."

"I scared the crap out of myself."

"It didn't show. Holmes said he's never seen anyone face down an enemy with the calm and courage you did."

"Appearances can be deceiving."

"What do you need from me?" he asked.

"You don't have to feel like you need to do anything. I can ask Rachel if she has another room, or I can find a couch to sleep on."

Eddy frowned at her. "What the hell are you talking about?"

"I won't make a scene. We can fight this evil thing coming and then go our separate ways."

"Are you saying you no longer want to be with me?"

"What? No! I'm saying you shouldn't feel obligated…"

He shook his head. "The only obligation I'm feeling right now is to turn that ass of yours a delightful shade of pink. Now, put your hands against the countertop, step back and spread your feet shoulder-width apart."

"I just fought the minions of whatever is coming…"

"And won without so much as messing up your hair. What you also did was blatantly disobey me, and for the record, I don't give a shit that it was in front of our friends. What I do give a shit about is that you took it into your head to do something dangerous without even bothering to talk to me about it. That is not okay. Since I can only assume you wouldn't know that would get you spanked, I'm going to go easier on you than I ever will again. Now, get into position."

She searched his face. She needed and wanted comfort, yet Eddy was going to spank her. Well, maybe he deserved at least that. She turned and put her hands on the counter, leveling her back and submitting her ass to his discipline.

Before she could prepare herself, his hand smacked her ass, the sound echoing off the tiled walls. She didn't have time to catch her breath or utter a sound before his hand came down again and began to rain hellfire all over her backside.

Tears welled in her eyes, and she moaned as the heat and pain flared across her buttocks and then seemed to sink in. She wasn't sure how many times he spanked her and knew it didn't matter. She knew that he would give her no more or no less than she needed and deserved.

There was something about the way Eddy spanked her, pain and pleasure twisting together and morphing into something new and exponentially more intoxicating than either by themselves. She realized in that moment how much she needed him. Needed him to take control so that if—no, not if, but when—she had to do something like this again, he would be there to pick up the pieces and see that it didn't shatter her soul.

The pace of the spanking slowed. She felt each and every blow distinctively. Each time his hand struck, he would hold it against her flesh, containing the heat and seeming to press it into her body. He spanked the back of her thighs and up where her ass met her legs. Corinne tried to keep from crying. She wanted him to be proud of her for being able to hold it together, but she was having to chew her bottom lip to keep from giving in.

"It's all right, Corinne. I'm here. I love you. I will take care of you."

If he'd yelled or even sounded disappointed, she could have held it together, but this was more than she could bear. The tears started to fall. She could lose control because Eddy was there to keep her safe.

"That's right. You don't have to always be brave. You can be afraid. I know how scared you must have been. But I also know it wasn't for yourself that you feared, but for our friends. So, you did what you felt needed to be done."

Corinne turned and clung to him and sobbed into his shirt. She was not a pretty crier—her nose ran, her eyes turned red, and her face turned blotchy, but Eddy didn't seem to mind or even notice.

"I didn't want to die. We didn't think there would be anyone here yet, if they were coming at all."

"I know, sweetheart, and maybe we should have given more consideration to you and Saoirse's arguments, but we didn't. We're men and we're flawed. We make mistakes, but regardless—if you ever disobey me again, that nice pink glow that's staining your backside will become a serious shade of red. Do you understand me?"

"Yes, Sir… Wait… What did you say?"

"That if you disobey me again, I'll give you a spanking you won't forget anytime soon."

"No, before that."

"That I understood…"

"No, before that. The mushy French stuff."

Eddy look confused but then recognition set in, and he grinned. "You heard that, did you?" She nodded. "I love you."

"Say it again."

"I love you. I love you. I love you. And if you *ever* doubt that, I'll lay so many welts across your ass you won't be able to tell where one begins and another ends."

"Yes, Sir."

"Corinne?"

"Yes, Sir?"

"I don't just like saying the mushy French stuff; I like hearing it too."

"We'll have to work on that, but I promise to tell you how much I love you every single day."

Eddy laughed. "And how much is that?"

"More. I love you more."

"*Bien*. Pull some clothes on and let's go back downstairs."

"I don't think that I'm going to be able to sit down."

"Not with any degree of comfort…"

"Won't they be able to tell?" she asked in dismay.

"Probably. That's the part that makes us even for them all knowing you disobeyed me. You don't want anyone to know you got disciplined? Then don't act out when there are others around. *N'est-ce pas?*"

"Yes, Sir."

She hated to admit it, but that did seem fair. She pulled her hair up into a high ponytail and pulled on some clothes. They rejoined their friends, who had ordered Chinese.

Eddy sat in one of the wingback chairs and tossed a pillow onto the ground beneath his feet. Without a word passing between them, Corinne sank onto the pillow between his legs and laid her head on his thigh as she'd seen Rachel do with Holmes. Eddy's hand immediately came to rest on her head and stroke her hair. She found it far more soothing than she'd thought it might be.

Spense and Saoirse weren't with them yet, and she rather imagined Saoirse wouldn't be sitting too comfortably either. When they joined the rest of them, Spense drew Saoirse onto his lap and held her close. At first the witch's body language was stiff and angry, but gradually that gave way to acceptance, and she leaned against her husband.

"Corinne, you seemed to know that woman," said Roark, whose cuts and bruises had been addressed as had Spense's and Holmes'.

"Yes, she worked for my aunt as a caregiver. I knew my aunt was dying, but she took a sudden turn for the worse. It seemed odd at the time, but I had no reason to question it. As she was on hospice care, no one really questioned it."

"We can have the body exhumed to have an autopsy done to determine the true cause," offered Holmes.

"To what end?" asked Corinne. "It won't bring my aunt back, and the woman who did it is gone. Do any of you know who she was talking about?"

Spense nodded. "Saoirse is pretty sure she knows who's behind the whole thing."

"Morgan Le Fay."

"As in high priestess of Avalon, Mordred's mother, Arthur's half-sister?" asked Rachel.

"Spense said she said she served *she who bore the son*

of the king that was and will be again. The king who was and will be again is King Arthur, and Morgan Le Fay bore his bastard son."

"So why the hell does Morgan Le Fay want to release demons into the world?"

"Because she wants to rule here, and to do that she has to disrupt everything. Shattering the wall between this dimension and that of demons would sure as hell do that and create a power vacuum for her to rule the world."

"Why does she want the swords?" asked Gabe.

"According to legend, because only the swords have the power to defeat her," supplied Rachel.

"Who forged the swords?" asked Corinne.

"Some say an Avalonian elf; but I don't think elf magick is that strong. An elf might have forged them, but my guess is that Merlin imbued them with their power," said Saoirse.

"I hate to be a killjoy," said Sage, "but can we talk about anything other than dark magick, swords, beheadings, and the like? You know they say for writers, everything is grist for the mill. Problem is, if I tried to use any of this as a plot for a novel, people would say it was too far-fetched, proving the old axiom, *truth is stranger than fiction*."

Sitting together, talking about normal things, doing dishes and taking out the rubbish seemed to allow everyone to hit the reset button on their emotions and nerves. A hush fell over the house as they all sensed the approach of midnight. They watched the mantle clock, and Holmes went over to one of the heavy leaded glass windows and opened it to let in the night air and so that they could hear the sound of Big Ben's chimes.

The bell began to toll:

One.

Two.

Three.

Four.

Five.

Six.

Seven.

Eight.

Nine.

Ten.

Eleven.

Twelve.

They had almost breathed a collective sigh of relief, when…

Thirteen.

"That's it," said Eddy. "Corinne needs to put on her boots."

"I'll get the weapons," said Holmes. "Rachel, turn the SUV around."

Everyone scrambled, and they assembled at the SUV. Holmes, Gabe, Roark, Eddy, Saoirse and Corinne loaded into the large vehicle. Gabe turned to look at his wife as he closed the vehicle door.

"I'll be fine, Gabriel. I'll be waiting. I trust you to take care of this just the way you trusted Saoirse and me to handle Azrael and the Warder of the Tower," said Anne.

"I love you, Roark. You better make sure you come back to me," said Sage.

Holmes looked at Rachel. "I love you."

Saoirse hugged Spense before joining them. "You'd better be here when I get back. I have the banshees on speed-dial."

CHAPTER 23

They loaded into the SUV and sped off into the night, heading first for Trafalgar Square and then whatever destiny awaited them. Corinne squeezed Eddy's hand, grateful for the fact that whatever they were going to face, they would face it together. They pulled up to Nelson's statue and unloaded.

Eddy climbed to the base of Nelson's feet, strung Storm Shadow, notched an arrow and turned to face Big Ben. He held his hand down to help Saoirse join him. Dark clouds rolled in and covered the moon, crackling and rumbling with thunder and lightning.

"I believe that's your cue," Corinne called up to her as she went to stand in front of the lion her aunt had called Wellington.

Saoirse raised her hands and began to chant:

With this fog I blind from hearing and sight,
    All that doth occur this night.
I call upon the power of the Maidens and the Light
    To join with those that stand and fight.
To destroy the beasts that threaten to come through
    this crack in time
And destroy this evil before the clock begins to chime

Corinne raised her sword. "I call on the power of Galatine to release the mighty lion Wellington to join us in defeating whatever is coming through the clock face."

At first nothing happened, and her companions all looked to her. *What the hell am I supposed to do? This is my first time as a superhero.* Just as she was about to say it again, she saw the bronze on Wellington's left front toe begin to crack.

"Here we go," she called to the others.

The crack began to widen and heavy chunks of bronze began to fall away. Corinne jumped back, just dodging a particularly heavy piece of the metal casing as it fell from the top of his head, shattering with a tremendous crash as it hit the ground. She looked over her shoulder and saw that London traffic continued to move as if nothing were happening. Saoirse's spell was working.

What was once bronze now became covered with tawny-colored fur. The shell that had held Wellington as prisoner began to crumble and turn to dust as the great beast sat up, shook his head and then stood, lifting his snout to the sky and roared, calling to his companions to awaken and join them. The others remained still—their bronze cages intact. Shaking off the last of its gilded prison, the lion looked down at her.

"Who calls the Lions of Trafalgar Square to defend the city?" he said in perfectly good, BBC English.

"Um, I do," said Corinne. "I am the Sentinel of the Portal and wield Galatine, shadow sword to Excalibur."

The lion leaned down and sniffed her dismissively. "Do you now?" he mocked.

Corinne brought the pommel down on the lion's toe with considerable strength, and it snatched its injured paw away. "Damn straight I do. Look, Wellington, I've never done this, and my guess is it's been a while since any of you were let loose. My companions are with me. One wields Courechouse, another Storm Shadow, and two more a quarterstaff and a halberd that my aunt bequeathed to me."

"We thought the other swords of Arthur's knights had been lost to time," Wellington said, taking a seat. "And you think to defeat those who serve the Faery Queen?"

"I thought she was the High Priestess of Avalon?"

Wellington snorted, and the puff of air from its nostrils staggered Corinne. "That girl always did have delusions of grandeur. I suppose she's sending forth her evil spawn."

"I haven't a clue. I'm walking into this blind. My aunt was dying when she finally told me the story. My friends have offered to help. Will you and your companions join with us to save the city?"

Wellington looked down at her, to her companions and back toward the other lions who remained still and encased in bronze. "Do you think to ride us like we are some kind of beasts of burden?" he asked angrily.

"Look, Wellington. You and the other lions are the fastest way to get from here to Big Ben. You're more than twenty feet tall and weigh seven tons. Are you really going to notice some puny humans sitting on your backs? But we do have the weapons, and we are prepared to fight with you. In addition to those who will go to the Clock Tower, we have a powerful witch and another warrior, who wields Storm Shadow. Will you help us?"

Suddenly the great beast roared again, the sound being drowned out by splitting and falling bronze as the other three lions came to life, snarling and shaking to free themselves. Wellington, Napoleon, Victory and Nelson all jumped down from their pillars and lined up in front of Corinne. They each leaned back and stretched out a front leg, bowing to her.

"We serve she who descended from Merlin and who fights for the Light. Gather your companions. We need to be away to the portal to join the battle," said Wellington, bowing down again so that she could walk up his leg and then, using his mane for leverage, climb to his back. Gabe, Holmes and Roark did the same, each mounting a different lion.

"It's up to you and Saoirse to hold them at bay until we get there," Corinne called to Eddy.

"We've got this. You should know getting killed is against the rules," shouted Eddy.

Corinne stowed Galatine in the scabbard strapped across her back and grasped Wellington's mane as the enormous lion galloped toward Big Ben. She could see arrows flying overhead in rapid succession and smiled. Not only was Eddy sexy, great in the sack and intelligent—the man knew how to shoot.

The four lions split up, each taking a different side of the enormous clock tower. It didn't take long for Corinne to hear the cracking of glass as some of the pieces of the clock face began to give way and fall. There was an enormous screech as a foul, black smoke was expelled and a dragon punched its way through, spewing fire and brimstone. Wellington roared a challenge and the dragon swooped down from the clock face to attack. It seemed to be focused on Corinne as Wellington leaped out of its way. As the dragon turned to follow, Corinne raised the sword above her head. Wellington sprang for its serpentine neck. Corinne brought the sword down, severing its head. The dragon's head fell as its body collapsed and vaporized. Corinne heaved a sigh of relief as she had feared it might sprout two more.

Behind her, Corinne heard a loud thunk as something heavy hit the ground. She turned to find herself facing not a dragon but an enormous being that looked like something out of a nightmare. The lower half of its body was that of a goat, the upper body was the muscular torso of a man, and its humanoid head had hard, curled protrusions growing from it like that of a big horn ram. It was mounted on some kind of demonic warhorse that breathed fire from its nostrils.

"I am Dragar," it shouted in a sound that was somewhere between a bleat and a cough—it was deep and raspy and its breath putrid. "Who are you?" it challenged angrily.

Corinne brought the sword up and across her body diagonally. "Me? I'm just a girl out for an evening stroll with her seven-ton lion."

I'm pretty sure sarcastic humor wasn't the way to answer this thing, but what the hell do I know? This is my first battle to save the world from demons.

"You will die, and I will feast on your heart," it snarled as it raised a short, curved sword and charged.

Seriously? Who writes this thing's dialog? Barely through the Veil and its already spouting cliches.

Corinne knew she should be more afraid of Dragar than she was, but it was so over-the-top, it was almost a caricature. She was terrified. The problem was her go-to defense seemed to be snark.

"I suggest you quit musing about your predicament and concentrate on the fact that Dragar means to kill you," suggested Wellington.

He had a point.

The horse's hooves sounded like thunder as it galloped towards them, bellowing its angry challenge. Wellington's roar drowned out the sounds all around them as he galloped towards the mounted demon. Both she and Wellington ducked as Dragar swept his sword at them trying to decapitate them both.

Dragar and its mount were far more unwieldly than Wellington. They lacked the great lion's grace and power. Wellington coiled around and launched himself toward the large equine, landing on its powerful rump. The horse might have been able to kick Wellington off, if the lion's sharp claws hadn't impaled it, knocking it and Dragar to the ground.

The satyr-like beast rolled away from the firebreathing equine before Dragar could be crushed. One swipe of Wellington's lethal paw ended the warhorse's suffering. Getting to its feet, Dragar brandished its sword and ran toward them. Wellington wheeled towards the demon and Corinne brought her sword up. She didn't know what would actually kill a demon, but she was fairly certain that removing its head would do the trick. After all, she reasoned, it worked with the dragon.

As the demon leaped in the air, trying to reach Corinne atop Wellington's back, she ducked and allowed it to leap over them. It bellowed in outrage and turned again, rushing them with the intent to kill. Wellington charged in response. Holding the sword above her head, she brought Galatine down with every ounce of strength she possessed. Dragar's death scream was cut off as Corinne cleaved its head from its neck in one fell swoop. As with the dragon, both Dragar and its mount vaporized into nothing, leaving no trace of their existence behind.

"Well done," growled Wellington. "You and your friends just might be able to pull this off."

Corinne looked up at the face of the clock and saw it was frozen in place. The portal might be open only for thirteen minutes, but time seemed to have stopped or at least slowed to a crawl. That thirteen minutes in the lives of the rest of the world might be hours or days here where the battle was joined. For what felt like hours, the four lions, Corinne and her companions became ferocious weapons of war, challenging whatever came through the clock face again and again. They were keeping the foul creatures that sought to claw their way into the world at bay, but there didn't seem to be any shortage of them.

～

"Corinne!" Eddy called as he ran to join them—after all her Protector couldn't bloody well protect if he was half a mile away. He ran as fast as he could and made a mental note to thank Sage for making him a fitness buff as well as a computer geek. Corinne sat atop Wellington, looking every bit like some ancient Amazonian warrior. *God, she was magnificent.* "We need to go inside."

"We?" she called down.

"Yes. Saoirse gave me some stuff to send into the portal that she believes will close it sooner rather than later and then seal it. In close quarters, the bow isn't as effective as the sword and Saoirse believed you were needed."

Corinne only took a moment to acknowledge that she heard him before she and Wellington attacked another demon as it tried to make its way into the world of men and then she slipped from the great lion's back to follow Eddy.

Snatching open the door, Eddy began to sprint up the hundreds of steps, Corinne in his wake. They focused on each individual stair tread until they made it to the clock face that had cracked. He pulled a glass vial from the quiver still strapped to his back.

"No!" cried out a feminine voice, its owner standing on the interior scaffolding.

Eddy turned to see a woman dressed in dark purple, her silver tresses tumbling down all around her and an ethereal glow enveloping her. It was Morgan Le Fay. It could be no other.

"You will not stop me," she cried.

"Not me, perhaps, but Merlin's descendant will," he answered.

"That evil wizard," she spat.

"Evil? You trap him in a crystalline cage for millennia, turn Arthur's son against him, help him kill Arthur and seek to loose your demons on my world, and yet you call Merlin evil?" challenged Corinne.

"He raped my mother and had me banished to Avalon."

"No, he helped Uther do that so that Igraine could birth the king who was and will be again. Merlin was forced to serve a bad king but did so in the pursuit of good and Light. It was your jealousy and rage that turned you away from the Light and sent you into the Dark. It was you who embraced its evil and now seek to visit that evil on this realm."

All the while Corinne was engaged with Morgan, Eddy unbuckled his quiver and softly lowered it to the ground, withdrawing one of his remaining arrows as he did so.

"Merlin is trapped and cannot help you," Morgan said with an evil smile.

"All it takes to defeat evil is one archer with a good arrow," said Eddy.

"Your bow will do you no good in such close quarters," Morgan said, approaching him, sidling up until she was so close, he could feel her breath on his face.

"Depends on how you use it," he said, whipping the arrow from behind his back and plunging it up under her ribs into her dark heart.

Morgan screamed and clawed at him as he shoved her backward. She fell, grasping at air as she did so, trying to avoid the swirling mass of black primordial goo below. As he heard her hit, he stepped to the edge and began firing the last of his arrows that had been dipped in Saoirse's magick potion. Corinne stood beside him pouring what remained of it into the opening. They watched as the whirling black mass became smaller and smaller until it collapsed upon itself entirely and vanished.

"Go. Get back to Wellington and fight whatever's left. I can handle the clean-up."

Corinne kissed him hard and fast and then ran down the stairs. Eddy took the last of the arrows and fired it into the shattered clock face, watching as it repaired itself until it was whole once more.

When he'd finished, Eddy ran back down the stairs, wondering why on earth no one had ever installed a lift in this damn thing, emerging from the clock tower to see Corinne on the ground, faced off with a knight with a shock of white-blond hair. His armor had seen better days, blackened with soot and blood and dented as well. The visor from the helmet had been ripped away and what lay beyond only remotely resembled something human.

Corinne and her opponent were well matched, and their swords clashed and clanged as they hit and slid down the length of the blade again and again. The dizzying fight seemed to go on forever, but Eddy knew it was probably only a matter of moments. The fight was balanced, and it seemed that neither combatant could get the upper hand. Corinne began pounding on the demon knight's sword, advancing with each blow, beating him back with sheer will.

Suddenly Wellington was there. His great jaws opened, and he grabbed the knight by the head, shaking him violently as if he were a mere rag doll that the lion wanted to play with. The body was thrown aside, and Wellington dropped the head at Corinne's feet.

The four lions, three with their riders still on their backs, stood looking at Corinne.

"I don't know why you all keep looking at me. I'm just making this up as I go along," she said before turning to Eddy. "I take it Saoirse's concoction worked and the portal is sealed?"

"*Oui.*"

"He's French," said Wellington with a slight sneer.

"There is nothing wrong with being French," said the smallest of the lions, who Eddy assumed was Napoleon.

"There is everything wrong with being French," retorted Wellington.

"The portal is no longer a threat… at least for now. We even managed to banish Morgan Le Fay into the demon dimension with her minions."

Wellington bowed, extending his front leg. "Come along then, both of you. It's time we get back to Lord Nelson."

Corinne showed Eddy how to climb up onto the great beast's back. She glanced up at the clock face—not only had it sealed itself, but the time showed as just a couple of minutes past midnight. Eddy sat behind her with his arms wrapped around her as the enormous lions made short work of the distance between Big Ben and Trafalgar Square.

As the lions each took their place at Lord Nelson's feet, Corinne said, "It doesn't seem fair."

Wellington's eyes grew gentle and kind. "It has been our proud and noble duty to serve this country, and we will continue to do so."

As Saoirse began to release the spell, the cloud cover began to dissipate, and the bronze began creeping up the lions' bodies.

"It was an honor to have served with you and your comrades," said Wellington before the bronze once again completely encased his body.

"It doesn't seem right. They fought just as valiantly as we did," said Corinne.

Eddy wrapped his arms around her. "Perhaps

when they sleep, they go to a different dimension and once again roam the great grasslands that were their home."

The others joined them. "You know," said Gabe, "there was a time I thought a wild night was just indulging in too much kinky sex."

"Is there such a thing?" asked Holmes with a grin.

"I don't know," said Roark. "Let's go home to our wives and find out."

They loaded back into the SUV and headed back to Chelsea. It was hard to believe that for the rest of the world, little time had passed at all from the time they had heard the thirteenth chime until now. Dawn was a long way off.

Corinne was curled up next to Eddy. "Hey?" she said softly. "Can I hear some of that mushy stuff?"

"I thought you didn't like it."

"I changed my mind."

"I love you," he said nuzzling her neck,

"I love you more," she said with a sigh, knowing it was true.

∽

Time. They would have more time. He would no longer need to return to London to train the Sentinel of the Portal. She had risen to the challenge and sealed not only the portal, but with the help of the Protector, they had banished his oldest enemy into her own demon dimension. He could feel the tendrils of crystal wrapping around his legs, stealing away his ability to move and immobilizing him. Time. It was the one thing that would continue on until he was needed again.

~

Thank you for reading *Bound: Masters of the Savoy!* I've got some free bonus content for you! Sign up for my newsletter https://www.subscribepage.com/VIPlist22019. There is a special bonus scene, just for my subscribers. Signing up will also give you access to free books, plus let you hear about sales, exclusive previews and new releases first.

Want a sneak peak at the next installment of the Masters of the Savoy series? Turn the page for a First Look at RELEASE (coming March 10, 2022)

If you enjoyed this book we would love if you left a review, they make a huge difference for indie authors.

As always, my thanks to all of you for reading my books.

Take care of yourselves and each other.

. . .

Other books in the series
Masters of the Savoy
Advance
Negotiation
Submission
Contract
Bound
Release

FIRST LOOK - RELEASE

MASTERS OF THE SAVOY

The night was upon him. Tremayne could feel the shackles of the curse releasing their stony hold on him. For more than five centuries, Holden Tremayne had been confined to his own personal hell. There were times Tremayne could see a kind of poetic justice in damning him to a half life where he only *lived* during the darkest hours of the night while most others slept. It was then and only then that the granite cracked, crumbled and fell away, releasing him once more into the world.

But it was a world that had changed vastly from the time before. Before he had been cursed and damned to hold an eternal vigil through unstaring eyes, he had been one of the privileged. He'd lived as he pleased. The son of the Duke of Cornwall, his days had been filled with fighting, drinking and wenching, activities in which he had excelled. It was the last of those behaviors that had damned him to the existence he now endured.

The girl had been a tavern wench, nothing more than a casual dalliance—a one-time thing to ease the lust that was riding him hard after a day of hunting and drinking with his friends. He hadn't forced her to his bed, nor had he known she was a virgin until he shattered the shield of her maidenhood as he thrust up into her.

Six months later she'd appeared outside the castle walls, standing on the cliff as the wind off the ocean roared its fury with what he'd done. When Holden had refused to marry her—after all, he might have been the first, but he wasn't the last—she had backed to the edge of the precipice, extended her arms out to her sides and simply tumbled backward to her death.

That night her elder sister had appeared, lighting a great bonfire in the same spot. As the flames had spit and crackled, dancing with the stars and the storm that swirled all around her, she pointed to Holden and called:

> You who dimmed the light that shone
> Shall be forever cast in stone
> To watch by day
> And live by night

> Your cursed life can only be undone
> When your devotion to the Light has begun

Then the tower of fire seemed to explode, and when it settled again to nothing more than a beacon of light, the witch had disappeared.

ABOUT THE AUTHOR

Other books by Delta James: https://www.deltajames.com/

If you're looking for paranormal or contemporary erotic romance, you've found your new favorite author!

Alpha heroes find real love with feisty heroines in Delta James' sinfully sultry romances. Welcome to a world where true love conquers all and good triumphs over evil! Delta's stories are filled with erotic encounters of romance and discipline.

*****

If you're on Facebook, please join my closed group, Delta's Wayward Pack! Don't miss out on the book discussions, giveaways, early teasers and hot men!

https://www.facebook.com/groups/348982795738444

ALSO BY DELTA JAMES

Masters of the Savoy

Advance - https://books2read.com/advance

Negotiation – https://books2read.com/negotiate

Submission - https://books2read.com/submission1

Contract – https://books2read.com/contract1

Bound – https://books2read.com/bound3

Release - https://books2read.com/release-dj

Fated Legacy

Touch of Fate - https://books2read.com/legacytof

Touch of Darkness - https://books2read.com/legacytod

Touch of Light – https://books2read.com/legacytol

Touch of Fire – https://books2read.com/legacyfire

Touch of Ice – https://books2read.com/legacytoi

Touch of Destiny – https://books2read.com/legacydestiny

Syndicate Masters

The Bargain - https://books2read.com/thebargain

The Pact - https://books2read.com/thepact-dj

The Agreement – https://books2read.com/theagreement

The Understanding - https://books2read.com/theunderstanding

Masters of the Deep

Silent Predator - https://books2read.com/silentpredator

Fierce Predator – https://books2read.com/Fiercepredator

Savage Predator - books2read.com/savagepredator

Ghost Cat Canyon

Determined - https://books2read.com/ghostcatdetermined

Untamed - https://books2read.com/ghostcatuntamed

Bold - https://books2read.com/ghostcatbold

Fearless - https://books2read.com/ghostcatfearless

Strong - https://books2read.com/ghostcatstrong

Boxset - https://books2read.com/Ghostcatset

Tangled Vines

Corked – https://books2read.com/corked1

Uncorked - https://books2read.com/uncorked

Decanted - https://books2read.com/decanted

Breathe - https://books2read.com/breathe1

Full Bodied - https://books2read.com/fullbodied

Late Harvest - https://books2read.com/lateharvest

Boxset 1 – https://books2read.com/TVbox1

Boxset 2 – https://books2read.com/Tvbox2

Mulled Wine – https://books2read.com/mulledwine

Wild Mustang

Hampton - https://books2read.com/hamptonw

Mac - https://books2read.com/macw

Croft – https://books2read.com/newcroft-dj

Noah - https://books2read.com/newnoah-dj

Thom - https://books2read.com/newthom-dj

Reid - https://books2read.com/newreid-dj

Wayward Mates

Brought to Heel: https://books2read.com/u/m0w9P7

Marked and Mated: https://books2read.com/u/4DRNpO

Mastering His Mate: https://books2read.com/u/bxaYE6

Taking His Mate: https://books2read.com/u/4joarZ

Claimed and Mated: https://books2read.com/u/bPxorY

Claimed and Mastered: https://books2read.com/u/3LRvM0

Hunted and Claimed: https://books2read.com/u/bPQZ6d

Captured and Claimed: https://books2read.com/u/4A5Jk0

Printed in Great Britain
by Amazon